PRETEND I AM
SOMEONE YOU LIKE

Shome Dasgupta

Livingston Press
The University of West Alabama

ISBN 13: 978-1-60489-211-6, hardcover
ISBN 13: 978-1-60489-210-9, trade paper
ISBN: 1-60489-211-0, hardcover
ISBN: 1-60489-210-2, trade paper
Library of Congress Control Number 2018948008
Printed on acid-free paper
Printed in the United States of America by
Publishers Graphics

Hardcover binding by: HF Group
Typesetting and page layout: Sarah Coffey
Proofreading: Joe Taylor
Cover art: Amanda Nolin

ACKNOWLEDGMENTS

"Went The Bite" has appeared in *Puerto Del Sol*; "Truck" has appeared in
New Orleans Review; "The Wandering Goat" has appeared in *Redivider*;
"Pepper And The Sun" has appeared in *NANO Fiction*; "Tongue,
Tongue, Tongue," "The Good Dead Dog," and "Rodeo" have appeared
in *Rougarou*; "Mud" and "Gone Went The Rabbit" have appeared in
Uncanny Valley; "We Were Together," "We Were Bowling Each Other,"
"We (Aluminum Tongues)," and "Magic" have appeared in *Peripheral
Surveys*; "Pecan" has appeared in *Used Furniture Review*; "Crawfish
And A Drawing By Barn," and "The Storm Was Coming" have appeared
in *Deep South Magazine*.

first edition
6 5 4 3 3 2 1

PRETEND I AM SOMEONE YOU LIKE

Thanks, Luke Sonnier.

A STABBING IN THE HAY

Rain, rain, rain, went the drop. Sink, sink, sink, went the drip. Wipe, wipe, wipe went the squeak, and blood, blood, blood, went the head. Woosh. And Barn, Barn, Barn went the woosh. Bird, bird, bird went the soar; machine, machine, machine, went the cling and clang; house, house, house went the fire.

Ting.

Song, song, song, went the sing, and breath, breath, breath went the fuck—bed, bed, bed went the springs, up and down, up and down, up and down, until wind, wind, wind, went the blow, coming through the window.

Morning suns—an infinite moment trapped in one second, penetrating pores until bodies were helium balloons, floating in the sky, like Barn.

Barn, Barn, Barn, went the float. Ice, ice, ice, went the crunch—hammer, hammer, hammer went the hit.

There were horses. There was a bear. There were animals.

Cow, cow, cow, went the moo, and cat, cat, cat went the meow, and dog, dog, dog, went the bark, and tree, tree, tree, went the sap.

There were buzzes and workers, and they went bee, bee, bee, and ant, ant, ant. Bee, bee, bee, went the ant, and rose, rose, rose, went the blossom.

Marigolds.

Bronze fields covered in gray—there were people there, walking fro and to and from there to here, and Barn could see all of them and point and laugh and shout and cry, until the people were gone.

When it's night, stars, stars, stars, went the glow, and meteor, meteor, meteor, went the shower, and Barn, Barn, Barn went the oooooooo.

Knife, knife, knife went the stab. There were blades. Shine, shine, shine, went the sparkle.

Barn was on the roof again—he had a jar of jellybeans and a bowl of feathers and a tube of glue. I went up there.

Barn, I said. I said, You're on the roof.

Pepper. Pepper, Pepper, Pepper went the sprinkle. Pepper slapped me in the face last week. I asked her why, and she slapped me again. Every time she slapped me, I wanted to kiss her.

Barn, I said. I said, You're on the roof.

Barn covered himself in glue and stuck feathers to his skin. He took one jellybean out of the jar and threw it until it became one with the sky.

Barn, I said. I said, Don't do it. I said, You can't fly.

He looked at me, watery and grinning.

Pepper was pretty.

The first time I saw Pepper was at the bowling alley. She was bowling alone, and I was there stealing relish from the condiment bar. She saw me stuffing my pockets and came up to me and asked me if I wanted to bowl with her.

No, I said. I said, I'm hungry.

Pepper said, I can put that relish to use.

Pepper said she would cook for me if I bowled one game with her.

When I went to her place after the game, she didn't cook for me, but I spent the night with her. Her legs were open the whole time, and I didn't have any clothes on until I left the next morning.

After that, Pepper and I weren't friends, but we slept together every weekend. Sometimes, I would go bowl with her, but she didn't cook any food for me as she had promised. I cooked for her, though—pasta, pizza, roasted chicken, and stuffed bell peppers were some of her favorites. I didn't like the way I cooked, but if she liked it, it made me happy.

Barn liked Pepper. He never really said anything about her, but when she would come over to pick me up, Barn would pretend that he was a gentleman and open every door and window in the house for her. Pepper liked him. Pepper didn't like me, not yet, at least.

I convinced Barn not to jump off the roof. Instead, he shared some jellybeans with me, while throwing some into the sky. He pulled off the feathers from his skin. It made his eyes watery.

Maybe one day, I said. I said, Barn. I said, Maybe one day you can fly and never come back.

Barn liked the idea. He stared into the clouds until he hypnotized himself and fell backwards with his eyes closed.

Pepper pulled into the driveway. She waved at us. Barn was still sleeping. I nudged him until he rolled over, and when he woke up, he had the imprint of a roof shingle on his face.

Barn, I said. I said, Pepper.

Barn peered over the roof and waved. He jumped from the roof to the nearby oak and scrambled down like a squirrel.

Barn, I said. I said, Use the chimney next time. I said, you can hurt your knuckles and elbows doing that.

I followed my own advice and climbed down the chimney. Ma was sleeping in the living room, sitting on the recliner. She had a plate of eggs on her lap and a cigarette in her mouth. I rocked the recliner, and she snored louder. I tapped her forehead, and Ma woke up.

Eat your lettuce, Ma said.

I said, I ate it already.

Where's Barn's nose, she said.

I said, it's on his face.

Good, Ma said.

I met Pepper in the front yard. She had Barn in a headlock.

Want to fuck, she said.

I nodded my head.

Barn was breathing hard. He spat in Pepper's face. Pepper hit him on the back of the head. Barn smiled.

That's impolite, I said to Barn.

Let him be, Pepper said.

Barn was already staring at the clouds again. He twirled around in circles and fell to the ground—he rolled around in the yard, covering himself with bits of grass. He stopped. His eyes were closed.

Pepper, I said. I said, Barn.

Pepper picked Barn up and brushed the grass off his skin and kissed him on the forehead.

Pepper's place was out in the field, just like our place. She didn't have a farm or a barn or anything, but there was green all around it, and the nearest neighbors were a good bit away. Pepper's place was full of dirt and mud and weeds. Pepper's place was like the field.

3

Me and Pepper were in her bedroom. I kissed her until my tongue was covered in the sweat from her skin. She grabbed me and jerked me around and the world spun, making me dizzy enough to grab on to the bedposts so I didn't fall off. Pepper had her mouth full. And then I had my mouth full. Our mouths were full of each other, and when we were finished, we stared at the ceiling fan until it stopped spinning.

Fan, fan, fan went the spinning. Tongue, tongue, tongue went the licks. Nipples, nipples, nipples went the hard, and uh, uh, uh, went the ah. Sheets, sheets, sheets went the wet, and wrap, wrap, wrap went the bodies.

I used the bed sheets to wipe the back of my neck. Pepper was wrapped in a pillow case. I slept on her. When I woke up, Pepper was staring at me.

Who are you, Pepper said.

I said, Pretend I am someone you like.

Why are you here, Pepper said.

I said, To make you feel good. I said, Do you feel good.

I don't feel anything, Pepper said.

I said, Good.

SUPERHERO

When Barn was four years old, this was three years ago, I took him to the Go And Go convenience store to buy a carton of juice. Barn's favorite flavor was strawberry-banana. This was when Barn talked—or at least, spoke in broken words. He was always a curious boy, not in the way of always asking questions but in the way of always looking at things and smelling them and looking at things and trying to understand them through silence.

His dad was there—Ma's brother, my Uncle Gerald. He was her only sibling. Uncle Gerald was wearing a black leather jacket, and his favorite torn jeans. When Barn saw him, he ran up to him and hugged his knee, but Uncle Gerald pushed him away. It was summer outside and the air was sticky, but Uncle Gerald was wearing a gray ski mask.

Uncle Gerald, I said. I said, It's hot. I said, How come you're wearing that hot hat.

He walked to the counter, pulling down the hat over his face.

Barn said, Superhero.

I said, Oh no.

Uncle Gerald pulled out a pistol and shouted. He asked for everything in the register.

Barn jumped up and down.

The cashier did as he said and gave him all the money. As Uncle Gerald walked out, he looked at me.

Uncle Gerald said, Don't tell my sister.

I said, I sure will tell Ma. I said, She's going to be disappointed.

Uncle Gerald was gone. Barn pressed his face against the window of the convenience store.

Pow, pow, pow, Barn said.

Those were Barn's last words.

Police, police, police, went the sirens. Lights, lights, lights, went the blue and red. Barn pointed at them. I told the officers everything they needed to know.

Thank you for your cooperation, one officer said.

I said, You're not welcome.

Barn knew something, I thought. He knew something was wrong, I thought. He was still very playful, that day, but he didn't say anything, like he was hiding his sadness. He didn't say anything at all.

The last time we saw Uncle Gerald was in court. As they were

5

taking him away, Barn ran up to him and patted him on the leg.

I don't want to see you, Uncle Gerald said.

And that was it. Barn stayed with us—me and Ma. His own ma wasn't around. She left Louisiana for Florida to be with a man who wouldn't go to jail all the time. Uncle Gerald was taken to a place somewhere in St. Francisville. Robbery wasn't the only thing he was charged with. He also beat up a man. He also beat up another man. He also shot people. Uncle Gerald wasn't going to be around for a while.

Barn, I said. I said, Why don't you talk anymore.

Barn would just sigh when I asked him that.

Is it because of your dad, I said.

Barn would just look at the sky.

There was something about him. Barn. There was something about him that looked for freedom. I felt that way sometimes, but I knew I was never going anywhere. But something about Barn's silence made him a powerful child. Like destiny. Ma loved Barn like she loved me. She treated us okay, and we treated her okay, except for the occasional tantrums I would throw at her. Barn never caused any problems though. He always kept me calm, too, when I was ready to explode.

I'm an adult now, I told myself. I told myself, I got to be grown for Barn.

It was like Barn was grown for me, though.

My dad, Pierre, left Louisiana seventeen years ago, when I was five. He went to Texas to get away from us. Ma said that he didn't like us—he never did, and he never would, so it was better that he left. I didn't mind much because I didn't like Dad too much, either, especially when he would kick us out of the house so he could give women money.

We were in the backyard.

Barn, I said. I said, How come you don't talk anymore.

I asked him that every morning. Maybe, one day, Barn would answer me.

Barn didn't say anything.

I said, Barn. I said, Say something.

Barn poked at my face and played with my cheeks, squishing them, moving them up and down.

What are you doing to my face, I said.

He put his hands over my eyes and then he pressed down on my nose. It made me sneeze. Barn jumped.

Pepper stood in the middle of a field. She wore a yellow dress. Short. I looked at her thighs.

Why are you so pretty, I said.

Pepper wasn't paying attention to me. Her hands were behind her head, like she was being arrested. She was coughing. I patted her on the back. She slapped me in the face.

Don't touch me, Pepper said.

She took off her dress, and in her underwear, she stuck one of her hands inside of her. She told me to take off my clothes. I did. Then, I was inside of her.

Do you think we can be friends, I said.

Pepper said, Never.

Pepper didn't have any friends. She lived alone.

How come, I said.

You're no good, Pepper said.

How come, I said.

Because you're here with me, she said.

I said, But I want to be here with you.

That's not good, Pepper said.

Pepper didn't have a background. There was nothing there behind her. It was just her, and that was all I knew about her.

Let's get some sno-cones, Pepper said.

In her truck, Pepper was still naked.

Shouldn't you put on some clothes, I said.

Don't feel like wearing clothes today, she said. She said, Feeling suffocated.

At the sno-cone stand, I got a spearmint one and Pepper got a strawberry one. She stayed in the truck. We ate them in the parking lot. I got one for Barn, too.

I should get this to Barn, I said.

It was a coconut flavored one.

We went to my house. Barn was in the tree. I could only see his legs—the other branches hid the rest of his body.

Barn, I said. I said, Coconut.

Pepper was in the front yard, too, still naked, with her hands on her hips. Ma came out the door.

Pepper, Ma said. Ma said, Where are your clothes.

It's hot, Pepper said. Pepper said, I don't want any today.

The mailman came by our house and stared at Pepper. He dropped all of our envelopes onto the street and drove off, almost hitting the stop sign at the corner of the street.

Ma said, You're causing trouble Pepper. Ma said, Come inside and get something to eat. Ma said, I got a pecan pie brewing.

Barn, I said. I said, Coconut.

A t-shirt fell from the tree. Then shoes. Then socks.

I said, Barn. I said, Keep your clothes on.

His pants fell to the ground, and then his underwear.

Barn, I said. I said, The bark is going to scratch your skin. I said, Coconut.

Barn climbed down the tree and tripped over one of the roots. He got back up and put his hands on his waist. Pepper scratched her arm. Barn scratched his arm. Pepper scratched her leg. Barn scratched his leg. Barn started running and tapped Pepper on the hip, and continued to run in circles in the front yard.

Tag, Pepper said.

She chased Barn around the yard and tapped him on the back.

You're it, Pepper said.

Barn turned around and started chasing Pepper. I went inside the house with Ma. She pulled out the pie from the oven and cut a slice for me. Pecan. I put some vanilla ice cream on top and watched it melt into the pecan sap.

Pepper, Ma said. Ma said, She's something.

I said, This is good pie.

She's a wild one, Ma said.

The vanilla makes my tongue tingle, I said.

Maybe she can get Barn to talk, Ma said.

I said, Pecan.

Pepper and Barn walked in, covered in grass and bites.

Pepper said, We fell into an ant pile.

Wash it off, Ma said.

Barn was trying to scratch his back but he couldn't reach. Pepper told Barn to go wash off first. She came up to the kitchen table and looked at the pie. I gave her a bite. She closed her eyes as she chewed.

MUD

Thunder, thunder, thunder, went the field. Crash, crash, crash, went the hay, and lightning, lightning, lightning went the bolts, and Pepper, Pepper, Pepper went the jumps. She stood on top of a cylinder of hay, in the middle of the rain, with her arms across her breasts, and her legs covered in mud, and jumped off and ran and jumped on another bale. She did this over and over again, after every lightning strike, trying to reach the next one before the thunder struck.

Pepper said, Let the lightning crash.

Crash.

The thunder struck and Pepper fell to the ground. I ran to her. She made mud angels. I jumped on top of her and made the same motions. She pushed her tongue against my eyes, and then she pushed me away and turned around, with her belly facing the ground. She stuck her tongue into the mud and moved it around. She stuck her fingers into the mud and moved them around. She moved her body up and down like she was fucking the earth.

Jealous, she said.

I did the same thing.

I said, Jealous.

Yes, Pepper said.

She slid over and grabbed me with one arm. With her other, she continued to finger the earth. I stuck my fingers into her with one hand, and the other twirled inside the mud.

Your first threesome, Pepper said.

I said, I don't know.

It's your first one with me, she said. She said, With us.

She licked the earth and then she licked me, and I closed my eyes and fucked everything around me. The lightning roared. The thunder was a whip, and when it lashed, Pepper would press down on me harder.

I said, You're scared.

Only when the rain stops, Pepper said.

We climbed on top of a bale of hay and continued. My semen was disguised in the rain, and Pepper looked at me.

Who are you, she said.

I said, Pretend I am someone you like.

Pepper was on the floor. Pepper was covered in blood. Pepper was crying.

How come you're like that, I said.

She said, shut up.

I can clean you up, I said.

Go, she said.

Pepper looked broken. I sat down next to her. Her place was messed up. There were shattered lamps. Her TV screen was cracked. Her toaster was dented. Her couch looked like it had been moved from its original spot. Her rug was scrunched up, and there was a hole in her wall.

Who did you fight, I said.

She said, Shut up.

How come you're crying, I said.

She said, Always take care of Barn. She said, No matter what. She said, You make sure he makes it through life okay.

He takes care of me, I said.

She started to bang the back of her head against the wall. I put my hand behind her so that her head hit my palm rather than the wood. I went to the bathroom and got some toilet paper and tampons and used them to clean her up.

I said, There aren't any Band-Aids.

Pepper sneezed and blood came out of her nose. She put some toilet pepper in her nostrils.

She said, I'm a mess.

You're a mess, I said. I said, Should I try to beat up someone.

Pepper said, You wouldn't last more than five seconds.

I can fight, I said.

Pepper slapped me in the face. It was a hard one—throbbing and stinging.

Sneeze, sneeze, sneeze went the achoo. Hand, hand, hand, went the slap. World, world, world, went the twirl and cry, cry, cry, went the tears.

I kissed her on the cheek and she pushed me away and then she pulled me towards her. Her eyebrows were all scratched up. Her cheekbones were swollen.

I said, Ice.

Pepper rubbed her stomach and groaned.

I said, Why are you hurt.

Just take care of Barn, Pepper said.

Barn moved his hands across Pepper's face. Her eyes were closed. He moved them across her cheeks, her nose, her eyes and forehead. Barn put his hands on each side of Pepper's face and looked straight into her eyes. Pepper looked down and then she looked into Barn's eyes. Her hands were on top of Barn's hands.

Pepper said, I'm okay.

Barn took her hands and placed them on top of his head and moved them around. He went to the wall and banged his head against it—Pepper ran to him and pulled him away. Barn had small eyes. Pepper pressed his head against her chest.

Pepper said, Quit it. She said, That's not nice.

I lifted Barn up and twirled him around.

Whirrrrr, I said.

Barn's eyes were closed. I put him down and picked up Pepper—she hit me on the shoulder. I twirled her around.

Whirrrr, I said.

She punched me in the face and I put her back down. Barn was running in circles. Pepper ran in circles following him. Or he was following her. I joined. We were running in circles. Barn became dizzy first and fell to the ground. It was just me and Pepper. We ran for five minutes.

Ma shouted from the other room.

Good exercise, She said. She said, That's good.

Pepper tripped me and I fell face first. Barn jumped on me. Pepper jumped on me. We wrestled until I couldn't breathe anymore and gave in. Barn kissed me on the cheek. Pepper kissed Barn on the cheek. I kissed Barn and Pepper on the cheek. There was rain.

Pepper's face was still bruised and scabbed. She looked like a warrior.

Pepper said, Don't say anything. She said, I don't want to hear anything.

I kept quiet and looked at her lips.

Ma, I said. I said, Call Barn in for dinner.

Barn ran out of the room.

It was just me and Pepper.

EVERYTHING WAS GONE AND EVERYTHING WAS THERE

I closed my eyes and no one was there. I opened my eyes and they were all there. I closed my eyes and everything was gone. I opened my eyes and I saw everyone. I closed my eyes, and there was darkness. I opened my eyes and the world was before me. I closed my eyes and I was lost. I opened my eyes, and there was everyone.

I closed my eyes and dreamt. I opened my eyes and saw my dreams. I closed my eyes. I opened my eyes. I closed my eyes. I opened my eyes.

I closed my eyes and I was lonely. I opened my eyes and I felt like I should be there. I closed my eyes and I missed her. I opened my eyes and I missed her. I closed my eyes and saw Barn. I opened my eyes and saw Barn. I closed my eyes and we were all dead. I opened my eyes and cried. I closed my eyes and Pepper slapped me. I opened my eyes and Pepper slapped me.

I closed my eyes and I was hungry. I opened my eyes and Ma was in the garden. I closed my eyes and flew into the sky, and I kept going until my skin fell off. I opened my eyes and saw the field. I closed my eyes and I was gone. I opened my eyes, and I was there. I closed my eyes, and I was gone. I opened my eyes and I was here. I closed my eyes and saw bones. I opened my eyes and saw blood. I closed my eyes and saw the roof. I opened my eyes and saw Barn in the clouds.

I closed my eyes and felt nothing. I opened my eyes and felt nothing. I closed my eyes and felt nothing. I opened my eyes and felt flesh. I closed my eyes and she was there. I opened my eyes, and she was there. I closed my eyes, and I closed my eyes. I opened my eyes, and I opened my eyes.

I closed my eyes. I opened them. This was my world. There was a world, and we were in it sometimes. And sometimes, there was another world, and we weren't there. We had these worlds in our heads—Ma, Barn, Pepper, and me, and maybe all of these worlds could rotate around each other just like they do with the sun. Worlds, and worlds, and worlds, and we stood on them, and we stood on each other.

TONGUE, TONGUE, TONGUE

Shaker, shaker, shaker, went the salt. Eggs, eggs, eggs, went the chew. Ketchup, ketchup, ketchup went the bottle. Barn, Barn, Barn, went Barn.

At the grocery store, Barn stared at the box of pancake mix. Pepper was in the frozen foods section—she was looking for something that she could make for me. Barn picked up the box and moved it around in circles. He looked at the back and then held it up above his head.

I said, Do you want pancakes for dinner.

Barn jumped up and down. I put it in the shopping cart. Pepper walked up holding a box of frozen waffles.

Pepper said, We're thinking the same thing, Barn.

Barn wrapped his arms around Pepper's leg. She put him in the shopping cart and he stood inside like he was captain of the ship, pointing this way and that, directing traffic through the aisles. I couldn't help but imagine him wearing a cape. He was in the air, arms ahead of him like Superman, holding a box of pancake mix in one hand and a box of waffles in the other hand.

One day you will fly, I said.

Pepper looked at me.

What, she said.

I said, What. I said, Did I say that out loud.

Pepper looked at Barn.

Pepper said, Can you fly.

Barn looked around the grocery store. He looked up and down.

Pepper said, You can fly.

Barn looked at me with large eyes. I had put hope into his mind. He jumped out of the cart and ran down the aisles, trying to fly. Everyone was staring at him. Me and Pepper didn't do anything. I didn't know why Pepper didn't do anything, but I didn't do anything because somewhere inside of me, I thought that maybe be would be able to fly. Fly away from the grocery store, from this city, to the sky, and keep going until he melted the sun.

We eventually made it to the checkout counter. There was this man standing two people behind us. Pepper kept looking at him. He had a black mustache and dirty skin. His flannel shirt was tightly tucked in, revealing his gut slightly hanging over his waist. Raisin skin. Pepper pushed up against me. I pushed against

13

her. He looked at us and smiled. I didn't like the smile. It wasn't a good smile. It was a smile that came from darkness. Where was darkness? It was an indescribable place where the wrong smiles existed. Pepper squeezed my hand until it hurt. Barn was stuffing candy into his pockets until I told him to stop and put them back on the rack.

The man walked up to us. Pepper's nails were deep into my skin. The man walked up to us, and Pepper's nails were deep into my skin. Pepper's nails were deep into my skin as the man walked up to us. Pepper's nails walked up to us as the man was deep into my skin. Pepper walked up to us. The man's nails were deep into my skin. My skin walked up to us, and Pepper's nails were deep into the man's skin. The man's skin was deep into my nails, and Pepper walked up to us.

Pepper, the man said.

Pepper didn't say anything.

The man said, Pepper.

Okay, Pepper said.

The man pulled down his hat a bit and looked at me. He stuck out his hand. I didn't move mine.

How's your Pops, the man said.

Let's go, Pepper said.

Barn was playing hopscotch with the tiles on the floor. I told him we're going and he grabbed onto Pepper's leg as we walked away. The grocer looked at us and shouted.

Emergency, I said.

Barn jumped to the floor. I had to pick him up.

I didn't ask Pepper about the guy. I didn't want to get punched or slapped. I knew better. She didn't let go of my arm until we were in the car.

I need to put my seatbelt on, I said.

She said, Put it on.

I need my arm, I said.

She let go.

Barn was spitting in the backseat.

I said, Don't spit.

Barn started hitting his head against the back of my seat.

Pepper turned around and calmed him down. She just looked at him and smiled. Barn stopped.

We went back to my house. Ma was in the living room covered in yarn. She didn't know how to knit, but it never stopped her

14

from trying.

Where's the groceries, Ma said.

I said, There was a mix-up.

Pepper said, It's my fault. She said, we'll go back tomorrow.

Ma said, Hmmm.

Barn tapped his finger against his head.

What are you thinking about, Pepper said.

Barn ran to his room.

I told Pepper that I would take her back to her place. She said she wanted to walk. I told her it's too far for a walk and not too safe at night. Ma said I was right and lit a cigarette. Barn came back with PlayClay and put it on the center table. He started eating it.

Ma said, Barn.

I said, Barn.

Pepper said, How does it taste?

Barn stretched his arms out to say, this much.

I drove Pepper back to her place. We went to her room and she licked me. I licked her. We licked each other.

Tongue, tongue, tongue, went the lick. Salt, salt, salt, went the skin. Skin, skin, skin, went the spit. Legs, legs, legs, went the air. Mouth, mouth, mouth went the grunt. Close, close, close, went the eyes. Fingers, fingers, fingers, went the plunge, and stick, stick, stick, went the semen.

Pepper said, What's your name.

Mutty, I said.

Pepper said, Why are you here.

Pepper, I said.

Mutty, Pepper said. She said, Do I love you.

No, I said. I said, No.

Pepper wrapped herself inside the comforter. I fell off the bed.

I was picking up the groceries that we left at the store the other day. The Dirty Man was there again. He was wearing the same clothes. This time, he was holding something in his hand. It looked like it belonged inside an engine. My cart was full. My head was full. My pockets were full. I was thinking about Pepper. The Dirty Man walked up to me, but I didn't look at him. The Dirty Man walked up to me again, and I looked at him.

Pepper, he said.

I said, No.

You're friends, The Dirty Man said. Maybe more than that, The Dirty Man said.

I said, Just keep to yourself. I said, Just keep to yourself.

She's no good for you, The Dirty Man said. She's good for me, The Dirty Man said. Good money, The Dirty Man said.

The Dirty Man raised his head and laughed, and there was spit coming from his mouth, and there were grits in his stubble.

We were standing in front of the checkout counter, but we weren't in line. The Dirty Man was pushed aside. I pushed him. I pushed him and kept walking—Ma needed denture glue. The Dirty Man grabbed my shoulder and swung me around.

You don't do that, The Dirty Man said.

I thought about stabbing him in the gut, and I thought about him being on the floor and all.

You tell Pepper, The Dirty Man said. I'm here, The Dirty Man said. The Dirty Man said, You tell Pepper I'll be seeing her.

I said, It looks like she doesn't want anything to do with you.

It's not up to her, The Dirty Man said. The Dirty Man said, She's mine. Ask her Pops, The Dirty Man said.

Shin, shin, shin, went the kick. Dirty Man, Dirty Man, Dirty Man, went the ouch. Fuck, Fuck, Fuck, went the words. Knuckles, knuckles, knuckles, went the fist. Floor, Floor, Floor, went I. Red, red, red, went the shirt. Crowd, crowd, crowd, went the whoa. Stand, stand, stand, went the legs. Knees, knees, knees, went the Dirty Man. Inside, inside, inside, went the testicles. Cheeks, cheeks, cheeks went the tears. Smell, smell, smell, went the pupils.

The Dirty Man stood up and tucked his shirt into his jeans. He had a little bit of blood on his face. One of the managers walked up and asked us to leave the store. I asked her if I could pay for the things in the cart before leaving as The Dirty Man left.

I said, I need to get denture glue.

Aisle seven, the manager said. Near the back, the manager said.

I said, Ma doesn't want to lose her teeth.

I hadn't seen Pepper in a while. She wasn't here and she wasn't there. It was just me and Barn. We were spending a lot of time together. Sometimes I would look at him and wonder if the world was ready for him. Whether he would decide to talk again or not, there was so much inside of him. Ma knew it, too. She never said anything to me, but I would catch her watching Barn sleep in the fireplace and she would be talking to herself about how Barn would become an astronaut and take over the universe.

Stars, stars, stars went the planets. Planets, planets, planets went the orbit. Orbit, orbit, orbit, went the spin. Spin, spin, spin, went the twirl. Twirl, twirl, twirl, went the rings. Rings, Rings, Rings, went the dust, and dust, dust, dust went everything.

There was something special between Barn and Pepper, too. Sometimes, I would picture her as his mother—maybe not my wife, but she was his mother and she would take care of him, and he would take care of her. Sometimes, I would picture myself within that house, but most of the time I wouldn't be there.

There, there, there, went the nowhere. Nothing, nothing, nothing, went me. Me, me, me, went air, and me, me, me, went gone. Fire, fire, fire, went the skin, and ash, ash, ash, went the body. Body, body, body went the death. Death, death, death went the life. Live, live, live, went the breath, and breath, breath, breath, went the tongue, and tongue, tongue, tongue, went us. Us, us, us went the went.

This was the place we lived in. Nothing was outlined or defined. Four people. Barn, Ma, Pepper, and me. That was all it was. Four people. It seemed so simple and uncomplicated, but the energy around us blended the crevices in my brain, and sometimes, my sense became lost on the minds of others—particularly, Barn.

Where was Pepper? Barn missed her, too.

See Barn jumping on the roof. See Barn hanging from a tree. See Barn digging up the garden. See Barn lifting his hands to the sky, running in circles and diving into the dirt. See Barn say nothing. Hear Barn say nothing. Say something Barn. See Barn take off his shirt and try to fly. See Barn see the bird. See Barn see his own memories. See Barn eat cereal and spit it out into the fireplace. See Barn looking for Pepper. See Barn in the ditch. See Barn in the levee. See Barn everywhere. See Barn pet an ant.

See Barn nowhere. See Barn in the sky. See Barn see himself. See Barn and Ma in the backyard burying raccoons. See Barn kiss a mosquito. See Barn sticking his leg into the toilet. See Barn sticking his hand in the microwave. Say something Barn, say something. See Barn enlightened by clouds. See Barn naked, trying to fit himself into the mailbox. See Barn taping and gluing Ma's dentures to the chickens. See Barn play hopscotch.

I had dreams—dreams that Barn wasn't here, but he was in a pillow case floating in the Gulf until he learned how to fly. And when he learned to fly, he would pick me and Ma and Pepper up and take us to a place where we didn't have to worry about anything.

Barn's dad sent him a letter once from prison. Ma didn't tell Barn. She didn't open it and read it. She fed it to a goat.

The goat died.

The goat died.

One time we all woke up and saw a horse in the yard. It wasn't our horse. It walked away, and we never saw or heard about it again. Barn had this look in his eye like he knew that this was something important.

What does that mean, I said.

Barn stood in the yard for more than two hours. Maybe he was waiting for the horse to come back, or maybe he was trying to figure it all out, or maybe he knew what it was all about and he was supposed to stand in the yard for more than two hours.

See the Dirty Man with his hand in his pants. See the Dirty Man's smirk. Hear the Dirty Man's chuckle. See the Dirty Man at the store. See the Dirty Man talk. See the Dirty Man at the place. See the Dirty Man in the barn. See the Dirty Man's head. See the Dirty Man kneeling on the ground. See the Dirty Man looking at himself in the mirror. See the Dirty Man's eyes. See the Dirty Man's belt buckle. See the Dirty Man's calluses. See the Dirty Man's dirty. Find the Dirty Man. Find the Dirty Man in the room. Find the Dirty Man naked. See the Dirty Man naked. Hear the Dirty Man's semen. See the Dirty Man on the road. Feel the Dirty Man's mud. Catch the Dirty Man. Hear the Dirty Man's fist. Strangle the Dirty Man. See the Dirty Man in the bathroom. See the Dirty Man and Pepper. See the Dirty Man and Barn. See the Dirty Man dead. See the Dirty Man's voice. See the Dirty Man's breath. See the Dirty Man's hooves. See the Dirty Man's paws. See the Dirty Man's whiskers. Kill the Dirty Man. See the Dirty Man kill. See the Dirty Man with legs spread apart. See the Dirty Man in boots. See the Dirty Man cry. Palm the Dirty Man. See the Dirty Man and Ma. See the Dirty Man swish mouthwash. Hear the Dirty Man's aftershave. Hear the Dirty Man lick his fingers. See the Dirty Man stick his fingers in his mouth. Dirty Man. Dirty Man. Dirty Man. Dirty Man.

THE WANDERING GOAT

See Pepper on the floor. See the humming. Hear Pepper on the floor. Hear the humming. Pepper was on the floor again. She had red speckles in her hair. There was a humming coming from the kitchen, but Pepper was on the floor. I looked at her hair and parted it and saw her red scalp. Her eyes were open. There was a humming coming from the kitchen. The kitchen buzzed. Buzzing. Pepper looked like she wasn't there—her eyes were open. They were covered with something thick and see through but there was a distance between me and her. Her arms were nowhere. They weren't in the air or by her side or anywhere else. Her legs were dripping. There was red dripping down her legs. I tried to cry. Buzzing. Humming. I shook Pepper a bit. I tapped her on the shoulder. I hugged her and talked to her, but Pepper wasn't there. Her skin looked pretty when she wasn't there—a mixture of roughness, clay, and grass. Her nostrils moved—her nose eroded the air around her and her fingers appeared. I sat her up against the wall.

There were 83 bees in the kitchen. Maybe not—I could've counted some of them twice—but it looked like there were 83 bees in the kitchen. It was pretty. They flew around in groups, hovering over the counter, or next to the sink, or around the toaster. It was the first time I saw her toaster. The bees looked at me and I scrunched my shoulders to my ears and walked in. The noise dug into my skin, my head, and all I could see was honey. Honey, everywhere—I stuck out my hand and let whatever happened, happen. I didn't feel any stings, but only bumps against my knuckles, wrists, and palms. They were laughing. I was on my knees, and the bees formed a circle around my waist. The kitchen window was open. And one by one they stung me, and I thought about Pepper.

Bee, bee, bee went the wings, and wings, wings, wings, went the buzz. Honey, honey, honey, went the microwave. Eyes, eyes, eyes, went the head. Tickle, tickle, tickle, went the legs. Thorax, thorax, thorax, went the tickle. Antennae, antennae, antennae, went the feel, and love, love, love went my skin. Blood, blood, blood, went Pepper, and Pepper, Pepper, Pepper, went the blood. Window, window, window, went the open. Green, green, green, went the outside. Inside, inside, inside, went the yellow. The bees were my blanket, and they stung me.

I took Pepper back home to Ma.

What the fuck, Ma said.

I said, It's Pepper.

Put her on the dinner table, Ma said.

I said, Where's Barn.

Ma went to her room and came back with a toolbox.

That used to be Dad's, I said.

Wrench, wrench, wrench went the head. Screwdriver, screwdriver, screwdriver, went the wrist. Hammer, hammer, hammer, went the neck. Nails, nails, nails, went the front yard.

Ma had thrown away all of his tools and made it a first aid kit. She pulled out all kinds of things like bandages, strings, needles, buttons, alcohol, pills, hangers, popsicle sticks, candles, teddy bears, underwear, rolling pins, salt and pepper shakers, construction paper, duct tape, and refrigerator magnets.

I went and looked for Barn. His foot was stuck in the toilet bowl again. He was hopping on one leg trying to pull the other one out while one hand was rubbing his belly and the other hand was patting his own head.

I said, Flush. I said, Barn.

Barn pushed the lever down and as the water swirled, I swooped Barn up and twirled him around. He burped.

I said, Go see Pepper.

Ma took good care of her. She fixed her up and made her look like a mummy. She was sitting on the couch in the living room. Barn took out his crayons and started coloring her bandages. Ma asked her what happened, but Pepper didn't answer her. She kept her attention towards Barn.

If this happens again, Ma said. I'm going to call the police, Ma said.

I caught her eyes, and it was the first time they looked like that—like they were looking at me, asking for something. I went and sat next to her. She put her arm around mine.

I said, There were bees.

Bees, Pepper said.

I said, They were stinging.

They're supposed to, Pepper said. Pepper said, That's their way of showing love to you.

I said, Humming.

They saved my life, Pepper said. Pepper said, And you, too.

22

She moved her fingers around the bumps on my neck. Ma gave me some lotion. Barn was doing handstands. I told Pepper that she was staying with us for the night. She was already asleep on my shoulder. I moved aside and watched her sleep on the couch. Her hands were between her knees and her nostrils flared as she breathed out through her nose. Barn pinched it with his fingers, causing Pepper to breathe through her mouth.

I said, Let her sleep.

Pepper started to snore. Barn burped again. Ma lit a cigarette and blew the smoke into the drain of the sink.

Eat carrots, Ma said.

Orange, orange, orange, they went. Cuts, cuts, cuts, went the snore. Toilet, toilet, toilet, went the foot. Barn, Barn, Barn, went the throat. Ma, Ma, Ma, went Ma.

That night I stayed in the living room with Pepper. Barn was there too, sleeping in the fireplace. Pepper didn't budge. She didn't turn her body and adjust herself to get into a more comfortable spot. She was motionless, but there was something that made her look so alive. The deader she looked, the livelier I saw her. I sat in the recliner and counted her breaths. It was during these quiet times, I liked being around—I liked being alive. The Dirty Man was on my mind, too.

Pepper woke up with a grimace the next morning. As I was about to open my mouth, she told me to shut up.

And thanks, Pepper said.

I said, We have oatmeal.

Barn was still in the fireplace, but Pepper sneezed and Barn jumped quickly to his feet, and then started running around the living room, before tripping over Ma's slippers. He saw that Pepper was awake and went straight to her. She pinched his nose and told him good morning. She said she needed to go back to her place to clean up. I said I was going with her.

There's nothing for you there, Pepper said.

I said, The bees. I said, And humming.

She let me go with her—Barn tugged on my waist.

I said, Maybe next time. I said, Today isn't a good day.

Pepper patted him on the head. Just as we were leaving, Ma entered the room with a cigarette in her mouth, and a pistol in her hand.

Here, Ma said. She said, Take this.

Is it loaded, Pepper said.

Ma said, The safety lock is on.

What are you doing with a gun, I said.

Pepper tucked the gun into her jeans.

You shoot, I said.

Pepper said, I do.

I said, How come.

Pepper said, My dad showed me how to when I was five.

I said, Where's your dad.

Pepper thanked Ma for taking care of her and told me to take her back to her place.

Ma, you got a gun for me, I said.

She laughed.

But Ma, I said. I'm being serious, I said.

Ma said, Your gun is Pepper. Ma said, Keep her by your side.

I looked at Pepper and she patted her hip.

Pepper walked into her place holding the pistol in her hand. She told me to wait outside until she said it was okay to go in. When I walked in, the place was trashed. I was so focused on Pepper and the blood and the bees, I didn't realize how it was so messed up. The bees were gone. She started picking up some of the things—lamps, plates, glasses, the TV parts, bottles, clothes, table bits—and threw them in the trash can, which was also cracked and coming apart.

Place, place, place went the broke. Wood, wood, wood, went the splinters. Bits, bits, bits, went the glass.

There was a goat. It walked through the front door and looked around.

I said, Do you want me to kick it.

Let it stay, Pepper said.

I said, Why is there a goat in the living room.

Maybe it needs some air conditioning, Pepper said.

The goat made a noise that made me jump. Pepper threw a cup at me, too. The goat walked in circles. The goat was observing. The goat picked up Pepper's underwear with its mouth. The goat stepped on the plates. The goat moved its head around.

It wants some love, Pepper said. Pepper said, Go pet it.

The goat shied away as I went up to it. Then it ran into me. Pepper threw another cup at me. She held out her hand. There were carrots. The goat ate. Pepper got a beer and poured it in a bowl and pushed it towards the goat. It drank.

I said, You're very hospitable.

The goat made another noise and ran out of the house.

Legs, legs, legs, went the goat. Waaauuu, waaauuu, waaauuu, went the goat.

I said, Drunk goat.

The goat knows, Pepper said. Pepper said, The goat knows what happened and ran away. Pepper said, It's not drunk. Pepper said, It's horrified.

She gave me a beer and we sat on the floor, against the wall, and drank. I asked Pepper what's been going on. I asked her why she's always beaten up and so secretive. Pepper shook her head and knocked the beer can out of my hand. And she threw hers across the room. And she stuck her hands down my pants. And I stuck my hands down her pants. And my hands were hers, and her hands were mine. We could still hear the goat outside.

We rolled around the floor. We rolled around the floor and stood up and went back down on the floor and leaned against the walls and our legs and arms were out the windows and our lips were bruised and bitten and our noses tilted this way and that way. When we woke up, Pepper was under the coffee table, and I was holding broken pieces of a lamp.

Do we know each other, Pepper said.

I said, We do.

Do we like each other, Pepper said.

I said, I don't know.

Do you like me, Pepper said.

I said, I do.

Do I like you, Pepper said.

I said, I don't think so.

Pepper said, Pretend.

The field was made of bronze. There was Barn, standing in the middle, trying to fly a kite. The wind was dead so he was using all of his breath to keep the kite afloat, but his lungs weren't strong enough. I tried to help him out and blow on it, too, but it didn't move. So Barn just ran with the kite dragging and skipping, being torn apart, and there was a pathway covered in bits and pieces of yellow. Barn let go of the kite and did frog jumps in a circular motion. He stuck his tongue out from time to time and swallowed flies. He dove head first into a clump of clay and his head went through—his legs kicking up and down. I pulled him out and lifted him and twirled him around, and as he went around I would get glimpses of the sun, and I pictured it speckled with pepper. After I put him down, he ran and tried to take off into the air. He landed stomach first onto the field. He tried seven times, and then ran back to me breathing hard and rubbing his elbows. There were scrapes and reds but he was a tough guy. Tougher than me.

There were cowbells. I sat on the hood of a tractor and thought about everything before me, whether I could see it or not. Where will Barn be? What will Barn be? Barn, say something, I thought. Barn, I thought, tell me everything. My legs burned with ant bites but I didn't move. It felt good. It made everything real. It made everything go away from what's real. I wanted to hold Pepper's hand. I wanted to make it all go away for her. The farm was good. The farm was always good. The chickens, cows, and goats, and pigs—they all behaved and lived. Ma's cooking was always good. Ma. Ma had done good for us. I wished that I could do something for her, for everyone, but all I could do was sit and watch Barn play under the pepper sprinkled sun.

Sometimes when Barn wasn't around and I would be sitting in the field, I would see him flying in the sky, just below the sun, as the sun itself was coming down to the end of the world. One hand would be rubbing his stomach and the other hand would be tapping the top of his head. This was the way he propelled himself, and as he would try to wave to me, he would drop down a bit before propelling himself again. I would wave back.

The sun was coming down, and the Draculas were making their way to skin. Barn tried to catch them and put them in his pocket, but he ended up killing them. They started coming to my neck and my arms—I guessed that they knew the ants had control of my legs—and I started to swat them away, but then I just let them be. Let them have their blood while they could. Without those mosquito bites, I wouldn't know where my skin ended and where the air began.

ONE CHICKEN AND THE
BELL AT THE DOOR

Bell, bell, bell went the open, and door, door, door, went the wood, and stand, stand, stand, went the dad, and mouth, mouth, mouth, went the drop, and legs, legs, legs, went the jeans, and shirt, shirt, shirt went the denim, and door, door, door went the shut, and shut, shut, shut, went the open.

Pierre was at the door. Pierre was at the door and there was a lady in jean shorts standing behind him. There was a lady in jean shorts and the clouds were moving fast. The clouds were moving fast, and there was a wind. The wind was wet. The wet wind sprinkled humidity onto our necks. I saw their necks, and they were damp. Pierre, the lady in jean shorts, the fast moving clouds, the wind, the humidity, and our necks were all in one place. Pierre stood at the door.

I need a chicken, Pierre said.

I said, Ma.

Mutty, Pierre said. Pierre said, Give me a chicken.

I said, Ma.

The lady in jean shorts rubbed the back of her neck. The lady in jean shorts lit a cigarette and scratched her thighs.

You have chickens, Pierre said. Pierre said, Give me one.

I said, Ma.

Ma came to the door holding a radio. She threw the radio at Pierre and missed and hit the lady in jean shorts, knocking the cigarette out of her mouth and causing her to stumble backwards.

Either way, Ma said.

Laurennette, Pierre said. Pierre said, Laurennette.

Ma took a framed picture off the wall—it was a painting of a basket of fruit—and threw it at Pierre. This time it landed, and the frame formed a collar around his neck. The picture was torn in the center and Pierre's head stuck out of it.

Laurennette, Pierre said. Pierre said, Laurennette.

Ma said, Mutty. She said, Mutty. She said, Does Pepper still have the pistol.

Pierre said, Pistol.

I said, She has it with her. I said, But Barn has a bow and arrow set. I said, And I have a lead pipe next to my bed.

Go get the bow and arrows, Ma said.

When I got back, Ma was still at the door facing Pierre and the lady in the jean shorts. It looked like no one had budged or said anything.

I said, Did I miss anything.

Ma said, Nothing.

The lady in the jean shorts coughed. Pierre took a step back.

Laurennette, Pierre said. He said, Give me a chicken.

Ma aimed the bow and arrow at Pierre.

The lady in the jean shorts said, Fuck.

Ma shot.

The lady in the jean shorts said, Fuck.

The lady in the jean shorts jumped.

Pierre said, Fuck.

The arrow was in his thigh.

I forgot to take in the wind factor, Ma said.

I said, Good shot.

Give me a chicken, Pierre said.

He pulled the arrow out of his thigh and gave it to the lady in the jean shorts. She twirled it around like a baton.

She said, I was on the cheerleading team.

Shut up, Ma said.

Pierre said, A chicken.

You're not getting any chickens, Ma said.

Pierre said, Just one.

Once you leave the house, you get nothing, Ma said.

Pierre said, We need money.

One chicken won't get you much, Ma said.

Pierre said, We need a chicken.

The lady in the jean shorts started doing a routine. She tossed the arrow into the air and clapped her hands, and when she caught it, she shifted her hips this way and that way and danced in place, mouthing words.

Bust it, the lady in the jean shorts said.

Pierre said, Hold on.

The lady in the jean shorts stopped cheerleading and lit a cigarette.

You've done real well, Ma said.

Pierre shook his head and shrugged his shoulders.

Pierre said, Whatever happened to that little boy Barn.

I jumped at Pierre and pushed him to the ground. Ma laughed.

Don't mention Barn at all, I said. I said, He's none of your business and if you do anything with him, I'll put an arrow in your eye.

Ma said, Go get the lead pipe.

Pierre stood up. The lady in the jean shorts puffed.

Don't think I don't know about Pepper, Pierre said.

I turned back around.

And don't think I don't know about her situation, Pierre said.

I said, Tell me.

Give me a chicken, Pierre said.

I looked at Ma.

Go get the lead pipe, Ma said.

I ran off and came back with the pipe and gave it to Ma. She tapped the pipe against the doorway.

You tell us, Ma said. Ma said, Or this pipe will go through your eye.

Come on now, Pierre said. Pierre said, Just one chicken, and I'll never come back.

Ma looked at the pipe and then at Pierre and then at me. Ma tapped the pipe against her foot. The lady in the jean shorts brushed the arrow against the grass of the front yard.

Those are nice lilies, the lady in the jean shorts said.

I said, What now, Ma.

Ma told me to go to the barn and get a chicken and just as I was leaving, Barn woke up from his nap and came to the front door. He rubbed his stomach and started doing jumping jacks.

Little boy Barn, Pierre said. Pierre said, Where's your daddy.

Barn looked around. He galloped around the front yard and stopped when he got to Pierre. He tapped Pierre's knee.

Too shay, the lady in the jean shorts said.

Pierre bent down and picked him up.

I said, Put him down.

Ma said, Put him down.

Barn didn't say anything. Pierre twirled him around.

Where's your daddy, Pierre said.

If I pushed Pierre again, Barn could get hurt. Ma, however, worked around that. She hit Pierre on the back of the knees, making him put Barn down before stumbling a few steps to get his balance.

Now, Pierre said. Pierre said, Laurennette. Pierre said, How about that chicken.

The lady in the jean shorts patted Barn on the head, and Barn rubbed his stomach. Barn didn't say anything. I picked him up and brought him back to the doorway.

I said, Go play stars.

Barn ran inside.

The boy has a good body under his head, Pierre said. Pierre said, He'll make a good cow keeper. Pierre said, You give me a chicken and I'll make a trade with you.

Ma told me to take Pierre to the chickens. She told me to give him one chicken.

And you tell him, Ma said. She said, Pierre. She said, You make the trade or I'll beat you like a runaway pig.

The lady in the jean shorts started to follow us.

Ma said, Skunk. She said, Skunk, you sit here in the front yard until they come back.

I'll be bored, the lady in the jean shorts said. The lady in the jean shorts said, And my name isn't Skunk.

Skunk, Ma said. She said, You sit there in the front yard and shut up.

The lady in the jean shorts did as she was told. She started singing. Ma gave me the lead pipe.

Ma said, If there's hassle, you keep the calm with this pipe.

Pierre followed me to the barn. I breathed in the smell of hay and mud and fertilizer. It soothed the nostrils, making me think about udders and plowing and burning sugar cane when I was a kid. We walked to the far corner, where the chickens were kept and caged.

Pierre said, I miss the smell of raw purity.

You miss nothing, I said.

Pierre tried to talk nice with me, asking me how I'd been doing and telling me how grown up I looked, but I didn't let him in. He knew nothing about me, and I wanted to keep it that way. We got to the corner. The horses were resting their hooves and the cows were still standing. I needed to let them out the next day.

Trade, I said.

Pierre said, Pepper. Pierre said, Pepper is a whore.

I slapped Pierre. Pierre slapped me.

Pierre said, None of that. Pierre said, Your Ma isn't here. Pierre said, You show me some respect.

I slapped Pierre. Pierre pushed me to the ground and pinned me.

Pierre said, She's a whore.

I tried to struggle out of his grasp, but Pierre was stronger than he looked—skinny framed and all—and he shifted all of his weight onto my hips.

Pierre said, Listen. Pierre said, I mean nothing wrong.

He moved aside and let me stand up. He had taken the pipe from me and kept it by his side. The horses stirred. The chickens were quiet. The cows were looking at us.

Pierre said, Her dad. Pierre said, Before I met Laurennette, before you were born, me and Pepper's dad used to pal up for these heists.

Pierre said, He's no good. Pierre said, He's worse than me—all the thoughts you and your ma have of me—he's worse. Pierre said, He's no good.

I brushed off my pants and looked at the lead pipe.

Pierre said, His name is Mallow. Pierre said, Mean Mallow Marsh.

I said, Where's he at.

Pierre said, Nowhere. Pierre said, He's on the hide. Pierre said, Too many after him.

I said, How do you know about all this. I said, How do you know about Pepper, now.

Pierre took out a can of dip and put some in his mouth. I smelled mint. I put some in my mouth and felt the burn against my gums. I buzzed and spat. Pierre spat.

Pierre said, Brody. Pierre said, Y'all fought.

Pierre spat. I spat and pushed the dip back into the corner of my mouth using my tongue. I spat. There was a small puddle of black spit next to us. Pierre spat.

I said, He wears a big buckle.

Pierre nodded.

I said, He looks red and sweaty.

Pierre nodded.

Pierre said, Grocery store. Pierre said, Y'all fought.

I said, The Dirty Man.

Pierre said, He was a part of the group. Pierre said, They still keep in touch. Pierre said, Brody told him he wanted in on Pepper.

Mallow was selling Pepper to Brody. Brody gave Mallow money, and Brody got pieces of Pepper. He got her skin and everything in between.

I said, Pepper fights.

Pierre said, She sure does. Pierre said, She hasn't given in yet.

Pierre said, Brody can never get past her bites and after he beats her, he's too out of it to fuck her.

I said, Pepper.

You're in no good, Pierre said. Pierre said, I'd stay out of it. Pierre said, I'm staying out of it, and you all stay out of it.

I said, Can't leave Pepper by herself. I said, She's a good girl.

Pierre told me that Mallow and The Dirty Man were wanted for all kinds of things, but The Dirty Man got away with it because no one really knew what he looked like and he had a lot of alias names. And Mallow was good at hiding but because he wasn't robbing as much, The Dirty Man gave him money for his daughter and whoever else Mallow was giving to him.

I said, Who's got the edge.

Brody, Pierre said. Most probably, Pierre said. He's got most of the control, Pierre said.

Pierre slapped the dirt off his jeans and rubbed his hands together. I didn't know if he was expecting a thank you or not but I didn't say anything.

I said, Let's get.

Let's get, Pierre said.

What did Pepper get herself into? But she really didn't get herself into it, she was basically born into it. What was she supposed to do? I didn't know much, but I did know that Pepper was a fighter and that she was tough and that she was going to find a way to get out of this. And I was going to help her.

Pierre walked ahead of me with a chicken clucking in his hand. When we got to the yard he had this big smile on his face. The lady in the jean shorts was still there and she stood up and wiped the palms of her hands against her tanned thighs.

Pierre said, Got a chicken. Pierre said, Honey.

The chicken moved its head around. I rubbed the back of its neck and whispered to it.

Be good, I said.

Pierre said, Let's get.

The lady in the jean shorts nodded her head at me.

Hospitality, the lady in the jean shorts said.

I kind of waved to her, not really knowing what I felt about her. I was sure Ma didn't like her too much. Probably just as much as she didn't like Pierre.

Pierre tipped his hat and started the engine. I could see Ma looking out the window, smoking a cigarette and sipping on a beer. Pierre waved to her. Ma didn't wave back. The car made all kinds of noises as it went away, and there was a lot of smoke coming out of its pipe.

Barn came running out and I picked him up and ran around the yard. He put his arms wide and he jutted his head out as far as possible. His eyes were closed and he was smiling big.

One day, I said.

Barn kept his eyes closed and I kept running around, hoping that maybe Barn would be able to lift off, just like a kite.

Me and Pepper played hide and seek at the power plant.

Me and Pepper licked each other in the chapel.

Me and Pepper played word games using mud.

Me and Pepper stared at the sun until we saw nothing but darkness.

Me and Pepper took Barn to the roller skating rink.

Me and Pepper caught catfish.

Me and Pepper stuck our tongues into each other's eyes.

Me and Pepper munched on cracklin and sausage.

Me and Pepper plowed the fields and sprinkled glitter onto the soil.

Me and Pepper rubbed jalapeños all over our skin and ran our mouths over each other's flesh until we cried.

Me and Pepper pretended to play chess.

Me and Pepper dissected road kill.

Me and Pepper threw caterpillars and hoped that they would fly.

Me and Pepper counted the frogs' croaks.

Pepper stood in the middle of the bronze and green with her arms lifted in the air. The way the sun was shining, I could only see bits and pieces of her because I had to keep my eyes more closed than opened. The cows were around us, chewing grass and glitter—they looked like mighty elephants.

Pepper slid her bare feet against the ground until they were all brown and dirty. She ran up to me and rubbed them against my legs. I cupped a pile of dirt and threw it on her. She ended up tripping me and pushing my face against the soil, telling me to suck in as much dirt as possible until I couldn't breathe anymore, and it was then, she told me, that I would understand breathing and worms. It was during these moments, under the sun and in the dirt, when I knew Pepper was lost. She was away from everything, and she only thought about how to fulfill the next second. And then the next second. And then the next second.

When I lifted my head and as I panted, trying to get as much air as possible, Pepper rubbed her tongue against my cheeks and kissed my lips and put more earth into my ears.

We are humans, Pepper said.

She started throwing cow dung at the sun.

We are eclipses, Pepper said.

She patted one of the cows and gave it grass.

We are stomachs, Pepper said.

She tore off her clothes and put her fingers inside herself.

We are raw, Pepper said.

She took off my clothes and guided my fingers to her hips.

We are roots and parts, Pepper said.

We stayed there until every bit of our skin was covered in earth.

A DRAWING BY BARN

Ma was in the back boiling crawfish. Pepper was on the tree swing, swinging away. Barn was in his room. I was in the kitchen making iced-tea.

Pepper came inside wearing shorts and a bra. I poured a glass of iced-tea for her. She sipped. She squeezed some lemon into it, patted me on the back, and went back outside. She was doing good. Ma was shouting from the backyard. The window was open letting the smell of red powder, potatoes, sausages, and crawfish into the house. I tried to eat the air. She was sweating and panting and smoking cigarettes. I handed her a glass of iced-tea. She asked for more lemons. I gave them to her. She patted me on the head.

Cauliflower, Ma said.

I handed her some through the window. She tossed it into the pot.

Get me that other bottle of spice, Ma said.

She poured the whole bottle into the pot. She wiped her forehead.

It's going to be hot, Ma said.

Pepper shouted from the front yard. She said, Can't be too hot for my tongue.

You never had my crawfish before, Ma said.

Pepper said, I can handle everything.

I'm not even close to being done yet, Ma said.

Pepper said, I bet you I can eat six pounds without taking a sip of anything. She said, And finish before any of y'all.

You'll have to clean up then, Ma said.

Pepper shouted. She said, And you'll owe me case of beer.

I went out to the backyard. The heat from the boiling pot made me close my eyes. I started to sweat just like Ma, whose own sweat was dripping down from her chin onto her feet. She was wearing her bright orange muumuu—it was soaked. I could feel my shirt stick to my back.

I said, You need help.

She said, Get me a towel, please.

I climbed back into the house through the back window and went to the closet. On my way back out, I stopped by Barn's room. He was on the floor, drawing on some construction paper. The paper was blue, and he was using a red crayon. Barn was on his stomach, his legs were up towards the ceiling, and his tongue stuck out.

I said, Barn. I said, You ready for Ma's crawfish.

Barn stood up and showed me his drawing. I went to him and took it from his hands. There were four figures. They weren't really stick figures, but they weren't really human figures either. One was in yellow. One was in red. One was in green. One was in orange. They were all pretty much the same height. Everyone was smiling. V-shaped birds and a purple sun were above them.

I said, Who are those people.

Barn jumped up and down and then twirled around in circles. He pointed at the green one and then gave me a hug.

I said, Is that me.

Barn tapped my stomach.

I said, Well. I said, I look better in this drawing than I do in real life.

Barn burped and smiled.

I said, Let's go show this to Ma and Pepper.

The summer sun was coming down. With the floodlights on, I could see Ma, still dripping in sweat—she was singing to herself, using the wooden stirring spoon as a microphone. She swayed back and forth and moved her head up and down. She was giving a nice performance to her audience—boiling crawfish.

I said, Ma.

She took the towel and wiped her hands on her muumuu. She put the towel around her head like a headband.

I said, Ma.

She took the picture. Barn was peering over the boiling pot—he started to sweat. He breathed in real hard and started coughing. Pepper came around the house from the front yard. The bugs never bothered her. Barn ran up to her and jumped into her arms and started to play with her hair. Pepper's breasts pushed up against her chest, and she saw me looking at them.

You like that, Pepper said.

I said, Look.

Pepper went up to Ma and looked at the drawing, which already had spots of sweat all over it. Barn tugged on Ma's muumuu. We all bent down. Ma pointed at the yellow one.

Ma said, Who's that.

Barn slapped Pepper's knee,

Pepper said, And it just looks like me, too. She said, Thanks.

Ma pointed at the green one. Barn slapped my knee.

Ma said, He looks a lot better in this drawing than in real life.

I tugged Ma's ear playfully. Pepper squeezed my hand. Ma pointed at the orange one.

Ma said, Now. She said, Is that me, Barny boy.

Barn showed his teeth. Ma kissed him on the cheek.

Ma said, And then the red one must be you.

Barn jumped and when he landed, he spread his feet apart. He stretched out his arms and clasped his hands, sticking out his index fingers. He did it again. Ma stood straight—her muumuu was almost dark because of the sweat. Pepper smacked a bug that was on the back of my neck.

Ma said, Barn. Ma said, Who's that.

Barn closed one eye and looked straight down his stretched arms like he was aiming. Barn was playing guns. Barn had drawn his dad.

Ma said, He still thinks about him.

Pepper said, Who.

I whispered to Pepper. Pepper whispered back.

She said, Your Uncle Gerald.

I nodded.

I said, His dad.

Ma started to crumple the paper but then she stopped and straightened it out.

Ma said, It's really pretty. She said, Mutty. She said, Put that on the refrigerator and come help me and Pepper put the crawfish on the table.

I said, Barn. I said, Come follow me to the kitchen.

After we put the picture on the refrigerator, we went back outside and covered the patio table in newspaper before pouring the crawfish all over it. They were bright red. They looked warlike. Barn held one up in the air and pretended it was flying. He held its claws out wide and swung it around his head.

Ma said, Eat up. She said, There's plenty here.

I can eat it all, Pepper said.

Ma didn't say anything for the rest of the night. I helped Barn peel his crawfish. Pepper looked like she was eating a crawfish a second. They were hot. My nose was dripping, my tongue was almost gone, and my shirt was soaked. The crawfish juice stung the small cuts on my fingers. It felt good. Pepper looked fine. She had won the bet she made with Ma but she didn't say anything about it. We all just talked about how good the crawfish tasted. I was breathing hard, trying to let the air soothe my burning taste buds. When we were done, Ma started to clean up.

I said, Ma. I said, You get some rest. I said, I'll clean this all up.

Ma looked around and rubbed her forehead—she patted me on the shoulder and walked inside.

I said, Barn. I said, Go wash up and then I'll read you a story.

Barn ran inside. Pepper put her arms around my waist and kissed my ear. She helped me clean up. In the kitchen, we were washing plates and glasses, and Pepper was humming something. I started to hum along with her. We were humming. I looked at Pepper's fingernails. They were long and covered in blue polish.

Why blue, I said.

Pepper said, It's something refreshing. Pepper said, I like it.

I like it, I said.

Pepper said, Blue makes me feel good. Pepper said, Just like the earth and its water.

We should go swimming sometime, I said.

Pepper said, And then we should go play in the mud.

Pepper made this sound that made me want to get inside of her. I kept looking at her bra and she kept looking at me looking at her bra.

Pepper said, You like that.

WE WERE BOWLING EACH OTHER

Lane, lane, lane went the grease. Gutter, gutter, gutter, went the bowl. Frame, frame, frame went the X. Light, light, light went the neon, and pop, pop, pop went the corn. Fingers, fingers, fingers, went the hands, and wrist, wrist, wrist, went the flip, and swing, swing, swing, went the arms. Dog, dog, dog, went the hot. Spare, spare, spare went the pin, and pin, pin, pin, went the fall, and strike, strike, strike went the ball, and shoes, shoes, shoes went the laces.

Our hands and faces were neon and the walls were glowing.

Hips, hips, hips went the hands and lashes, lashes, lashes, went the eyes. There was swirling and twists and lights. Car, car, car went the seat and door, door, door went the shake. Roof, roof, roof went the legs. Pant, pant, pant went the breath. Window, window, window went the audience. Curse, curse, curse went Pepper.

There was licking.

Palate, palate, palate went the tongue. Lips, lips, lips went the neck. Thighs, thighs, thighs went the face. Face, face, face went the creases. Up, up, up went the toes. Down, down, down went the belly.

The car alarm went off.

And loud, loud, loud went the machine. Machine, machine, machine went the off. Tire, tire, tire went the drive. Us, us, us went the parking lot.

Everything was blurry. The lanes blended with the sidewalks, and the cars were mixed with people, and the night—there wasn't any night. The stars fused together to form one big splendid sphere of twinkle.

Us, us, us went the bed. Pillow, pillow, pillow went the floor. Hair, hair, hair went the pull. Hands, hands, hands went the slap. Throat, throat, throat went the grunt. Throat, throat, throat went her mouth. Throat, throat, throat went the inside. Throat, throat, throat went the tip. Throat, throat, throat went the throat.

Nothing could be seen. My eyes were closed. She was everywhere.

Dive, dive, dive went the tongue. Muscle, muscle, muscle went the tongue. Tongue, tongue, tongue went the rub. Tongue, tongue, tongue went the tickle. Pound, pound, pound, went the hard.

Open eyes and open skin—she floated and jerked. A hot room, full of us, wavered. Night was inside with its wet body and we covered ourselves with each other. Sleep, sleep, sleep went the sweat.

BARN AND PEPPER AND THE SUN

Barn, he wore this cape, and he was in the air with one arm stretched forward and the other arm bent, resting on his back. Barn, he was in the air, tearing the air, with his cape coloring the air, with his eyes piercing the air. Barn, he flew towards the sun with a bit of sweat on the back of his neck, and he twirled and twisted, dizzying the rotation of the world as he maneuvered between clouds, racing birds, racing time, racing himself. He knew nothing but freedom. Barn, his blood flowed backwards and forwards and it circled around causing cyclones within his strands. His muscles, small and tight and neat—his stomach tucked like a metal sheet. He was in the air. Barn, he was in space, dodging stars, dancing on meteors, and he sneezed and blew the planets away. Barn, he was in space, the caped astronaut, polishing the rings. Light years and light years away—there were centuries and eons and the future blended with his fists and lips. Barn, he remained silent—curving the galaxies with fluid motion, wavelike, and the universe was just a glowing rock.

Pepper, she was on the sun. Pepper, she was sunspots. Pepper, she made the sun bigger—furious and spicy, the sun swallowed Pepper, wanting her, calling her, and the sun changed shapes and colors, and the sun started to sing. Pepper, she was singing. She sang, Pepper, and Pepper—she drove right in, forming tunnels and tornadoes, bright tornadoes, fiery tunnels, and loud caves. Pepper, she journeyed to the center of the sun, naked and dripping, with eyes closed. Pepper, jump-roping on the sun, and the sun, it ascended and descended in rhythm—Pepper, the sun's rose, pushed it up and down. Pepper, she bounced along, tumbling, cart-wheeling, and flipping, and the sun gave in and gave out. Pepper, she cried in the sun. Came morning, came night, Pepper was always there—flailing her arms, her breasts giving milk to the sun. Her breasts nurtured the sun. Her nipples singed the sun. Her hips and hands and hair, her knees and tongue, and her toes, were the sun. Pepper, she covered the sun with her body. Pepper, she fucked the sun and made the sun grunt and moan and she made the sun sleep. Pepper—the core of the sun, swimming in the sun's magma. The craters of the sun were Pepper. Pepper and the sun.

THE GOOD DEAD DOG

There was a dead dog on the road. The dead dog was on its side, its tongue stuck out, and its eyes were closed. It was a mutt. The dead dog's hair was matted and clumped and wet and torn. There were patches of pink and gray skin. The dead dog's gums were dark black—its teeth looked like they gave up a long time ago. The dead dog's paws blended with the dirt on the side of the road.

Pepper crouched down and smelled the dead dog. She had parked the truck on the side of the road to take a look at it. I stood behind her staring at the dead dog's tail, picturing it moving back and forth.

Pepper said, No wounds. She said, It wasn't hit by a car.

There were ants around the dead dog—Pepper brushed them away and told them to quit it.

Pepper said, Maybe old age. She said, Maybe something was hurting on the inside.

What about the other side, I said.

Pepper rolled the dead dog over. There were still no signs of any physical hurt.

Pepper said, Maybe starvation. She said, Maybe dehydration. She smelled her fingers.

She said, It smells like bubblegum.

The road was freshly paved—it was bright black, and there weren't any potholes. Cars and trucks and eighteen wheelers sped by on the back road. I looked at the back of Pepper's neck, wanting to lick it. She stood up and jogged to the back of her truck and after a lot of clinking and clacking and moving things around, she came back with a shovel.

Where at, I said.

She headed over to a field not too far from the road. There was a house farther down—land must belong to them, acres and acres. We didn't walk too far in, but Pepper made sure the spot was right for digging. She dug. She stuck the shovel into the earth, and bit by bit, she tossed the dirt aside. We took turns. Pepper was in her bra. Cars honked as they drove by. Pepper flicked all of them off. When she dug, I stared at her pink bra, watching her breasts move up and down and side to side—sweat trickled down the middle. She started to take off her bra.

44

Keep it on, I said. I said, You look pretty with the pink bra.

Pepper spat. She grabbed her breasts—she ran her hands down her body to her belly button. The field was making her feel this way.

Keep it on, I said.

Pepper panted.

I said, Another time.

Pepper licked the palms of her hands. I took the shovel from her and started digging. I dug. The dog lay dead. The sky turned gray, and there was the smell of rain. I looked down the road and saw a pale sheet. Pepper sat and rocked back and forth, trying hard not to dig her fingers into the soil, trying hard not to stick her tongue in clay. There were worms.

I said, Good soil.

It looks like it tastes good, Pepper said.

We dug and dug, about four feet in, and we lifted the dead dog and we put it in its grave.

Pepper said, Be good.

Her jeans were unbuttoned, but the zipper was still up. The sun was almost down, and the rain came. We stayed there. We patted the removed clumps of dirt and soil back on top of the dead dog. The dead dog looked happy. I thought I saw its tail move. I thought I saw its tongue move. Pepper tapped my back with the shovel. She threw the shovel away and tackled me. I couldn't get a hold of her and she had full control over me. She twisted my legs and arms. She rolled me over. The rain came down. The dead dog was in the earth. Pepper stood up and took off her bra. It was dark. Headlights zoomed by, making the raindrops look like lightning bugs. I took off my clothes. Pepper pulled down her jeans. There was nothing. There was nothing, and without saying anything, we ran across the wet field. My feet pushed down hard against the grass. Pepper was ahead of me, the grass didn't seem to slow her down at all. She was making sounds and noises with her mouth, babbling anything and everything—any thought, any word, any anything.

We stopped and looked around us.

There is no dog, Pepper said.

The dog is dead, I said.

Pepper said, Bury me.

When you're dead, I said.

Pepper said, Next to the dead dog.

45

Dog, dog, dog went the dead. Shovel, shovel, shovel, went the dig. Lights, lights, lights, went the head. Bra, bra, bra went the pink. Toe, toe, toe went the mud. Down, down, down went the rain. Hands, hands, hands went the body. Me, me, me went the mercy. Slash, slash, slash went the blades. Dark, dark, dark went the air, and air, air, air went the zoom.

There was wind, and it sparkled every now and then when the cars drove by. The cars and trucks and cars were silent in the rain. The rain was the loudest, and when we ran with the wind, it talked to us, and when we ran against the wind, it shouted.

Wheel, wheel, wheel went the cart. Frog, frog, frog went the leap. Knees, knees, knees went the ground, and body, body, body went the tumble, and blades, blades, blades went the tickle, and blades, blades, blades went the sharp.

Let's go home, Pepper said.

There were our clothes. Pepper walked past them. She turned around, back to me.

Leave them, Pepper said. She said, Leave them and come with me.

I said, Skin.

We left the dead dog, and we left our clothes. The rain still came down hard—Pepper drove with the windows down. I was shivering. Pepper was singing. The night was never-ending, and I never wanted it to end.

WENT FISHING FOR RABBITS

Ma said, Mutty.

She was on the red recliner in the living room. It squeaked as it went back and forth. She was reading the newspaper. Barn was outside. Pepper wasn't there. I was there.

Ma said, Mutty.

I poured a glass of iced-tea and gave it to her. Outside, through the window, there was a rabbit nibbling leaves in the garden.

Rabbit, I said.

Ma said, Don't let Barn see it.

How come, I said.

Ma said, He'll try to ride it like a horse. She said, Mutty. She said, Gerald.

He's gone, I said.

Ma said, He's gone.

Dead, I said.

Ma said, He's escaped. She said, There was a prison break yesterday morning in St. Francisville.

I said, He's coming.

Ma said, Barn.

Ma lit a cigarette and sighed and stopped rocking the recliner. Barn came through the window and ran up to Ma and tugged on her nose.

Ma said, Little one. She said, You know so much.

She hid the newspaper behind her back and put Barn on her lap and started rocking the recliner back and forth. I poured Barn a glass of milk. I gave Ma a beer after she finished the iced-tea. She chugged it down, and Barn tried to do the same thing with his milk but it went in too fast and he choked and spat some of it back out.

I said, Take your time.

I wiped his chin with my shirt and Barn took my hand and led me to the window. He climbed through and I followed him. Barn jumped to the ground, stomach first, and I did the same. He pointed at the rabbit.

I said, You can't ride. I said, It's too small.

He tip-toed to the garage and came back with a fishing pole. The rabbit was light brown, about the size of a football. It was chewing the leaves from the garden—there was basil and thyme and red peppers and eggplant. Usually, it was Barn chewing the garden.

Barn pulled the fishing pole back and then pushed it forward—the reel spun, making a quiet whirring sound, and the line landed just to the side of the rabbit.

I said, Good aim.

The rabbit ran off. Barn looked at me. I shrugged my shoulders. Barn reeled in the line and looked at the end of it.

I said, Fishing for rabbits. I said, It's tough.

He ran off into the end of the backyard, where the fence was lined with myrtle trees and the ground was covered with mulch and fallen leaves and branches. The rabbit was nowhere to be seen—just Barn, grazing his fingers against the fence, looking for the disappearing act. I went back inside.

Ma was on the phone. I hadn't seen her talk on one for a few months. She paced back and forth and sipped her beer. Her cigarette rested in an ashtray I had made when I was in grade school. She hung up the phone.

Police, Ma said. She said, I gave them a call.

She told them that she would call them if she heard anything about Uncle Gerald. I looked at the newspaper—there was a photo of him. He had a bald head—the last time we saw him, his hair came down just below his earlobes. His faced had thinned out, too, and there was a tattoo of a bright red crawfish on his neck. He had some good tasting boils, but Ma's were always better. She always got the spice right. Gerald learned a lot from his older sister—boiling crawfish, fishing, carpentry, and all, but he could never pass up Ma's skills. When he was around, whether we were at his place, or he was at our place, he was always asking questions and always watching every move Ma made. He had looked up to her back then, but then he got into these big dreams of living rich and got into crime. Somewhere in Ma's mind, I knew she believed that he took this kind of life to make things better for Ma after Pierre had left.

WENT THE BITE

We climbed up the water tower. The dome, from far away, always looked like some kind of spaceship ready to take off—ready to take over. It always looked fresh and dominating from far away—the smoothness of it, the round shape, the quietness about it, it was all soothing as it molded the sky around it.

Up close, it was dirty and rusted and chipping away. There was graffiti everywhere, beer bottles and cans and cigarette butts surrounded it. Condoms and brown lunch bags and unwound paper clips here and there—the spaceship was more like a dumping ground, a dull junkyard with no thoughts or dreams of flying away into the galaxy.

Pepper was a mess. Her eyes were full of red, and the skin underneath was dark and sinking, and there were scratches on her arms and bruises and bumps on her forehead and neck. I wondered if she'd had another run-in with The Dirty Man or if she had done this to herself. I still hadn't told her yet that I knew about her connection to The Dirty Man. She didn't know that Pierre had come over. Her breath was full of beer and she smoked cigarette after cigarette—a habit I didn't know she had—and wobbled back and forth against the railing of the water tower. She wasn't talking. Her head was somewhere else. She mumbled things every now and then, but I couldn't make any sense of it. I wasn't sure if she knew I was there with her.

I said, Pepper.

She turned her head towards me, still grabbing onto the railing.

I said, Maybe we should go back down.

Her head looked like it was about to come off, like the neck was just a string ready to give in. Her skin looked dead. Her cells looked dead. She was moving around and she looked dead. Pepper looked out over the railing and held up a beer bottle and tossed it over. There was a clank a bit later—a thud.

I said, I don't want to fall over. I said, I'm feeling kind of woozy being up here.

You got teeth, Pepper said. She said, You got teeth.

I said, I got teeth.

Show me your teeth, Pepper said.

I opened my mouth. She stuck her fingers in my mouth and rubbed them over my teeth while holding onto the rail with the

49

other hand. She touched each tooth with her index finger and her thumb like she was trying to pinch each one. Then she rubbed her finger against my gums. Her skin felt good.

Dogs got teeth, Pepper said.

She took her hand out of my mouth and rubbed her own teeth. You need teeth, Pepper said. She said, Dogs got teeth.

I said, You got teeth.

I stuck my fingers in her mouth and rubbed them against her teeth and her gums. She moved her tongue around them and bit down a bit but not hard.

Dogs can't bite without teeth, Pepper said. She said, A bitch needs good teeth.

There were helicopter sounds. We both looked up. If it wasn't for the helicopter, I wouldn't have noticed the sagging stars. They looked like they could be grabbed. I raised my hands but there was just air, and I almost fell over the railing. Pepper put her hands up, too and was grabbing air. Her head rocked back and she almost fell backwards.

I said, Hold on.

Sharp teeth, Pepper said.

The helicopter beats went away, and it was quiet again. The stars were quiet, and some were blinking.

Pepper started to bite her own skin. I tried to stop her, but she pushed me away, and again, I almost fell over. I wondered if I would survive if I went over the railing. There were teeth marks on her arms and she stuck them out. I bit on them, too, but not hard enough to break skin. I tasted her salt and her sweat.

I said, Thinking of jumping over.

Go, Pepper said. She said, You got teeth. She said, Just bite everything.

Holding onto the supportive wiring, I got up onto the railing. It got darker. I wondered. I thought about the broken pieces of bottle on the ground and how they would shred me up, dead or alive. It could all be gone. Barn. Ma. Pepper. The farm. It could all be nothing. How would it feel? How would nothing taste? My skin felt like it was lifting off my bones. I looked at Pepper. She was staring at me. Her eyes, still red, were gone—lost in me. She looked like she wanted to say something, but nothing came out. I saw her tongue. She coughed. She was staring at me. Her teeth were there.

Bitch, Pepper said.

I pictured Barn flying in and picking me up from the railing and setting me on top of the tower's dome. Could I make it? Dead didn't look so scary. It looked comforting. It looked like a bed. It looked like a swimming pool. It looked like Pepper's belly button. It looked like Barn's socks. Dead didn't look so scary. It looked like a pitcher of iced-tea. It looked like Ma's muumuu. It looked like a cow. I could be dead and happy.

Droop, droop, droop went the stars. Bird, bird, bird went the chop. Bottle, bottle, bottle went the pieces, and smoke, smoke, smoke went the ash. Pepper, Pepper, Pepper went the red. Air, air, air went the quiet. Gums, gums, gums went the teeth.

There were no dogs. There was just us.

Bitch, bitch, bitch went the bitch. Scabs, scabs, scabs, went the scratch, and scratch, scratch, scratch went the arms. Wrist, wrist, wrist, went the trickle. Bra, bra, bra went the sky. Skin, skin, skin went the bite. Skin, skin, skin went the sunk. Sink, sink, sink went the skin. Free, free, free went the thoughts. Up, up, up went the down. Down, down, down went the up, and cold, cold, cold went the hot. Hot, hot, hot went the hands. Shake, shake, shake went the wires.

The wires were stubborn.

Laces, laces, laces went the ground. Loud, loud, loud went Pepper. Knees, knees, knees went the bend.

What happened when there was nothing?

There was Barn.

Air and breath.

There was Ma.

Heart, went the pound.

There was Pepper.

Pepper was stray. Teeth. She had teeth.

I got back down. Pepper was in her underwear. Her bra was sinking in the air. She held my hand.

A bitch's teeth need water, Pepper said.

I said, There are bowls of water.

We have teeth, Pepper said.

She pulled my lips apart and licked my teeth. Her eyes were open. I kissed her teeth. She pulled my arms to her chest and I grabbed her breasts and moved them up and down and rubbed her nipples.

Calcium, Pepper said. She said, Gums.

Her nipples were hard. Her eyes were still red. The darkness around them looked faded.

I said, You're back.

I know you, Pepper said.

She pinched my tongue with her fingers. Her stomach was covered in beer.

Tongues are just as good as teeth, Pepper said.

She straddled the railing and moved back and forth, her hands around my waist.

Push me over, Pepper said.

I put my hands on the sides of her shoulders and held her tight. She leaned backwards, away from me, and tilted her head backwards, looking at the sky upside down.

The sky is just there, Pepper said. She said, It doesn't look too far.

Pepper straightened herself out and looked at me. Her nipples were still hard and on the side of her body was a large bruise— large enough to make me hurt and I felt a throbbing on the side of my stomach.

I prepared. I was trying to think ahead. I was trying to see into the future to make sure that no matter what she did, I would be there to make sure she wouldn't die. She pushed my arms aside and then pushed me and lunged backwards. She went for it. Her body was over the railing and she was on her way down, but I grabbed her foot with both arms. Pepper dangled.

String, Pepper said.

I said, Fuck Pepper.

I'm almost there, Pepper said.

I said, I got you.

This is taking forever, Pepper said.

Her feet were tiny, making it easy to keep my clasp. She had hit the back of her head against metal and there was blood dripping.

I said, Are you alive.

Pepper said, The blood made it. She said, My skin just needs to be with it.

I said, Fuck Pepper.

I pulled her feet up and over the railing. My stomach was burning. It looked like my arms had muscles. Pepper's breasts were upside down and moving this way and that way while at the same time pointing towards the ground. I leaned backwards and coughed and pulled her slowly back over the railing. Her skin squeaked against the railing. She started to flail her legs and arms.

I sped up and once her whole body was over the railing, I nudged her against the wall that led up to the dome, and she slid down against it and sat down, with her feet just reaching the free space under the railing. I looked up and focused on the space between the stars. Pepper's head was bleeding bad.

Let's get to the ladder, I said.

Pepper said, I'm hungry.

I said, I'll cook you something. I said, I'll bandage you up.

She rubbed the back of her head and looked at her fingers, covered in wet.

Pepper said, Teeth. Pepper said, Even a stray bitch can survive.

Are you a bitch, I said.

She barked.

Barn balled himself up and rolled around his bedroom in his underwear. Ma was in the living room staring out the front window. Her head was slightly tilted with a thumb covering her lips. It looked like Ma was thinking. She turned around and looked at me and then around the house. She looked at the ceiling, the roof, and the walls. She looked at the doors and pushed and pulled on knobs. She counted the windows and tested the attic door to see if it was still working. She walked out into the backyard and looked at the oak tree and then walked alongside the fence looking at the ground.

I said, Ma.

She came back inside and then walked through the front door and faced the house with her hands on her hips. She was thinking. She walked to the sides of the house and did the same thing.

I said, Ma.

She shut the door. She was still outside, and I was inside. It felt dark, and Ma's worried look and pacing were making me scared. Ma had never made me feel scared before. She wasn't doing it on purpose, though—she was doing it so that we wouldn't have to be scared.

Lock it, Ma said.

The door clicked. There was a loud bang and the door shook. There was a loud bang and the door shook. The knob twisted and rattled and then there was another bang. My head popped at every bang and my heart kept jumping. There was a knock.

The door clicked, and Ma walked through.

I said, Ma.

She walked into Barn's bedroom, where Barn was still rolling around. She looked at his window. Barn stopped rolling and stood up and watched Ma. Ma left. Barn went back to rolling around on the floor. She walked into my bedroom and did the same thing. She didn't go into her bedroom.

I said, Ma.

She went into the garage and shuffled some boxes around and opened the closed door. I put the garage light on. There was noise and something fell, making a shattering noise. There was more noise—boxes being moved around, things being taken out, and things being put back in. Ma came back out, holding two boxes stacked on top of each other.

There's a storm, Ma said.

I said, What kind of storm. I said, Hurricane.

It's coming, Ma said. Ma said, We'll be ready.

She put the two boxes on the kitchen table. She pulled out a hacksaw. She pulled out a bowling ball. She pulled out a carjack. She pulled out metals of different shapes and sizes. She pulled out and she pulled out. They were never-ending boxes. Ma's hands were at work. There was a rolling pin, Barn's old toys, two glass pitchers, a collection of closet hangers, Pierre's fishing box, and there were these things all on the kitchen floor. Ma started to hide them all around the house.

Watch where I put them, Ma said.

I watched and made notes. Behind the curtains. Under the sofa. Behind the TV. In the tub. Under the rugs. She taped the hangers on the wall. She used Pierre's old fishing lines and made trip-wires all around the house. She put a container of thumbnails between the washer and the dryer. I followed her into the backyard, and she hid unused forks and spoons in the garden, and hung buckets full of nails on the branches of the trees lining the fence. There was a cooler with some crawfish still in it. Ma pulled it around the corner of the house just next to Barn's window.

Ma said, We'll need those crawfish. Ma said, They're just as good dead.

Back inside the house, she opened the freezer and checked to make sure there were some bags of ice. There was also a box of frozen waffles, and a carton of ice-cream.

Ma said, Waffles.

Syrup, I said.

Ma said, Good idea.

She opened the fridge and took out the syrup.

Ma said, There's plenty. Ma said, We're set.

When's the storm coming, I said. I said, Hurricane.

Ma said, Soon. Ma said, When it's dark outside.

Barn ran out of his room and tripped over one of the wires Ma had set up.

Ma said, You watch out for those wires. She said, Just keep jumping.

Barn got right back up and started jumping around the house. His elbow was bleeding. He never cried. I never saw him cry. Barn didn't cry.

Shook, shook, shook went the house. Lights, lights, lights went the out. Door, door, door went the banging. Yard, yard, yard went the rustling. Wind, wind, wind went the air. Mouth, mouth, mouth went the shouts. Branches, branches, branches went the trees. Tails, tails, tails went the squirrels.

The windows were boarded and sealed.

Dark, dark, dark went the room. Eyes, eyes, eyes went Barn. Ash, ash, ash went Ma. Pepper, Pepper, Pepper went the smoke. Us, us, us went the wait. Crack, crack, crack went the creaks, and dog, dog, dog went the bark, and silent, silent, silent went the street.

We were all in the middle of the living room—Barn, Pepper, Ma, and me. The lights were out. We were surrounded by banging and clanking and shouting. I gave Barn a Discman and put the headphones around his ears, hoping that he wouldn't be able to hear all the loud noises. He would look around, though, and he jumped and clenched his body every time there was a sound. Ma was in her muumuu holding a carjack in one hand and a beer in the other and a cigarette loosely hung between her lips. Pepper came in just before all of this started. Ma gave her some of Barn's arrows, a butter-knife, and a screwdriver. I had a hammer and a rock.

Uncle Gerald was trying to get inside. He was shouting and cursing and hitting the house.

Sister, Uncle Gerald said. Uncle Gerald said, Let me in. He said, Don't do this to me. He said, You have my son. Uncle Gerald said, I am your brother.

Ma didn't say anything—she stood there in the living room just waiting. Her jaw looked loud and her eyes looked narrow.

I'll break the house, Uncle Gerald said. He said, I'll break the whole fucking house right now.

He was right outside the door. Pepper walked up to it and right when she got there, the door shook and banged, and she jumped back. I looked at Barn. His hands were over each side of the headphones, pressing them against his ears. I put the volume up for him.

Ma said, Pepper. Ma said, You got the pistol.

It's in the truck, Pepper said.

Ma said, Well. Ma said, At least the truck is ready to defend itself.

You'd shoot him, I said.

Ma said, Right in the calf. Ma said, Just to keep him down.

Pepper said, I can go get it. She said, If you distract him, I can sneak out.

We can't let Barn see him, Ma said. Not now and not like this, Ma said.

Barn hadn't shown any acknowledgment of recognizing Uncle Gerald's voice. It was difficult to—with all the shouting.

Voice, voice, voice went the roar.

The quickest way is through the back gate, Ma said.

Pepper said, Let's give him some attention on the other side. She blew smoke into her bra.

Barn needs to eat his dinner, Ma said.

I fixed him a plate of broccoli, peas, and fried chicken. Ma made him eat in the living room, sitting on the coffee table.

Just this once, Ma said.

She looked at me. I thought. I thought, and she looked at me. I told her that I would go out through the back and go to the other side of the house, not the side with the gate, and throw rocks at him.

Pepper looked at Ma.

Pepper said, And you stay here with Barn and I'll get the gun.

Ma nodded her head.

What's Plan B, Ma said.

We thought. We were in the living room. We thought and we were in the living room. As Pepper was opening her mouth to say something, there was banging against the back door. Ma had drilled boards over it just like when there was a hurricane. There was grunting. Underneath the boards, there were more boards. Ma made sure the back door was just as safe as the front door. Uncle Gerald was still shouting just outside the front door. There was banging on the back door.

Ma said, Surprise. Ma said, There's two. She said, Everyone stays in the house for now. She said, Pepper let the truck have the gun. She said, We'll hold our own without it.

Ma looked at Barn. He was twirling around with his headphones. He moved his hips side to side and started to dance.

What did you give him, Pepper said.

I said, Tupac.

Barn stood on top of the coffee table and started to do jumping-jacks. Ma told him to get back down. She turned towards me.

Ma said, Take Barn to the attic. She said, It's hot up there. She said, Make it cold.

I said, Barn. I said, Strip naked.

Barn took off his clothes, wearing only his underwear, and I put his shoes on for him.

Ma said, Take the cooler. Ma said, Take two of the flashlights up there, and a pillow and a blanket.

We found a good solid spot for Barn in the attic. The wood wouldn't give in, and it was away from all the machines and wires. One flashlight was on, and the other flashlight was kept off for backup.

I said, Barn. I said, This is an adventure.

Barn had never been up in the attic. He looked around as he would if we were at the zoo.

I said Barn. I said There aren't any giraffes here.

Below, I heard muffled shouting and clanking. I put the blanket down and gave him the pillow.

I said, Sleep.

Barn tugged on my finger. He lay down with his stomach facing the roof. I sang him a song. It was a song Ma used to sing to me about lightning bugs and dreams and farm animals and mosquitoes. There were alligators, too. Barn shut his eyes and shifted to the side of his body. I kissed him on the side of his head and made my way back to the attic door. I didn't want to turn around because I knew he would be looking at me.

I said, Go to sleep. I said, I'll be back.

I turned around. He opened his mouth, looking like he wanted to say something. This was the first time I didn't want him to say anything—to speak.

I said, Lullaby. I said, Sleep. I said, This is an adventure.

He gave me a thumbs up. I waved.

Downstairs, as I walked past Barn's room, a hand grabbed my arm and pulled me in. I grabbed throat.

Harder, Pepper said.

I squeezed a bit more. The thundering continued outside. It was hot inside—sweat dripped down. Pepper's neck was soaked. My thumb moved up and down against her skin.

Just for a second, Pepper said.

She put her hands down my pants and felt around. My hands

were now on her chest. I could barely see her face. I closed my eyes. My hands were underneath her bra. She had a clasp on me—her fingers talked to my skin. Her fingers smoothed out my skin. Her fingers morphed my skin. I pinched her stomach. I moved my hands in circles around her belly button. I kneeled down. Her jeans made a faint sound as they hit the floor. I was inside and I couldn't breathe. Pepper's sweat was on my shoulders, and she pulled my hair and whimpered. I took a deep breath and went in again. She pulled me up and she kneeled down and her mouth covered me, whole and wide, and with my hands on top of her head, I let the rhythm move them back and forth. She stopped.

Just for a second, Pepper said.

She stood up.

I said, Take your bra.

She strapped it around her chest.

I said, Ma must be wondering.

Pepper was still breathing hard. My heart had calmed down, and we walked out of the room and back into the living room. Ma was sitting on the sofa, drinking a beer and smoking a cigarette. When she exhaled, she made a soft sound like when she was blowing on a scraped knee or elbow.

I said, Ma.

The storm is still going, Ma said.

I said, They can't stay here forever.

My brother has great tenacity, Ma said.

The banging and clanging and shouting was still coming from both the front and the back.

I said, Neighbors.

They got to be wondering by now, Pepper said.

She took a cigarette from Ma's pack and lit it. The glow from their smokes was charcoal in a brewing grill. With each puff, I could get a sense of my surroundings. After each suck, the dark had control again. Every time the orange came back—like a stray cat's eyes in an empty parking lot—I felt this sense of invincibility and confidence. They smoked.

I said, Let's do something.

Ma said, Do something.

Barn, Barn, Barn went the attic. Lick, lick, lick went the neck. Sweat, sweat, sweat went the drip. Drip, drip, drip went the drop. Floor, floor, floor went the knees. House, house, house went the thunder. Wood, wood, wood went the board. Window, window,

window went the dark.

In between the quiet, there was cackling and howling—packs of voices and knuckles.

Room, room, room went the living. Puff, puff, puff went the smoke. Lips, lips, lips went the glasses. Ma, Ma, Ma went the forehead. Salt, salt, salt went Pepper. Salt, salt, salt went the potatoes.

We sat at the dinner table eating pork chops and mashed potatoes.

Ma said, The neighbors are too far away.

Pepper chewed. I sipped.

Pepper licked the bone. I chewed. My knees shook.

We washed the dishes.

Barn should be asleep by now, I said.

Ma said, Dreamland.

Pepper licked her lips—I could hear her scratching her back.

I said, Ready.

Ready, Ma said.

Pepper said, Ready.

Barn's room was near the driveway. His window was boarded only on the inside, to give us a way out. This was Ma thinking ahead. I was there. Pepper stood by the back door. Ma was at the front door. We all had our weapons. The flashlights were off. I had my hammer and screwdriver. Pepper had her lead pipe. Ma had her machine guns of nails, and wrenches and spoons. The living room floor was covered in frozen crawfish.

With my eyes closed I felt for the screws Ma had put into the board covering the window. There were two in each corner, and two in the middle at the top and two in the middle at the bottom. I turned them all left. Left, and left, and left until they were loosened. I had to be quiet. I used my fingers and took them out with one hand while the other hand held the board against the window. The screws tickled the floor. The board was off. I flickered my flashlight five times against hallway wall for Ma and Pepper to see. That was Step 1.

Croak, croak, croak went the croak. Croak, croak, croak went the croak. Croak, croak, croak went the croak, and croak, croak, croak went the croak.

There were frogs. The song of the frogs filled the house—they were loud and bulging, wanting to be heard. They sounded angry—full of scorn. Why? Sometimes while they were singing,

Barn would count every croak until he fell asleep, and when the frogs finally stopped, he would wake up and run outside to see where they had gone.

They're sleeping, I said. I said, Go to sleep.

Ma and Pepper had seen the flashes of the light against the wall, and they started banging against the walls and wooden boards and anything else that could be banged, like the coffee table, the kitchen table, the counters, the floor, and the cupboard.

Uncle Gerald stopped shouting and clanking. The other guy did the same. Pepper and Ma stopped hitting the house. There was silence. I stuck one leg out the window. Ma and Pepper started to hit the house again. Ma and Pepper started shouting. Uncle Gerald and the other guy started shouting. I slid across the grass to the driveway, to Pepper's truck. I went to the far side of the truck to keep hidden and opened the front passenger door. Pepper had said the pistol was in the glove compartment. A bottle of whiskey rolled out, onto the car floor, and there was a picture frame with a photo of me and her and Barn playing with the sprinkler. Ma must have taken it and given it to her. I wiped the smudge marks off and took a sip of the whiskey. There was the pistol. I put it in my pocket. As I closed the door and duck-walked back to the window, there was the lady in the jean shorts standing at the front of the truck.

I said, Pierre.

She was chewing gum and smoking a cigarette. She was smoking a cigarette and chewing gum. The straps of her tank-top were loose around her shoulders and drooped to the side, showing tan under the streetlights. She looked happy to see me—I felt like I was her longtime friend.

I said, Pierre got his chicken.

He's here with Gerald, the lady in the jean shorts said.

I said, How come.

Gerald needed some help, the lady in the jean shorts said.

I said, How come.

She looked around the shoulders. I went back and ducked behind the truck.

Gerald is a wanted man, the lady in the jean shorts said.

I said, He should go back to jail.

He wants to see Barn, the lady in the jean shorts said.

He's gone, I said.

She scratched her thigh. She scratched her elbow.

These frogs are angry about something, the lady in the jean shorts said.

I said, They don't like y'all.

They don't mean any wrong, the lady in the jean shorts said.

I said, He's a pit bull right now.

He just really wants to see Barn and your Ma and he's hungry and needs some sleep and he needs some time to think.

I said, He killed anyone else.

She shrugged her shoulders.

Pierre said that he's changed, said the lady in the jean shorts.

I said, I'm going back in.

They're around the back now, said the lady in the jean shorts.

I duck-walked back to the window and as I was climbing in, I felt hand around both of my legs.

I said, Fuck.

Son, Pierre said.

I said, Fuck.

Let us in, Pierre said.

I said, You got your chicken.

This is for Gerald, Pierre said. Your Uncle Gerald, Pierre said.

Uncle Gerald came up right behind Pierre.

What the fuck, Uncle Gerald said.

I said, Uncle.

He nudged Pierre aside and took my legs and pulled me back out.

I said, You need a chicken.

Where's your Ma, Uncle Gerald said.

I said, She went to visit you in prison but I guess she just missed you.

Uncle Gerald spat. Pierre spat. The lady in the jean shorts spat. I spat.

You got smart, Uncle Gerald said.

I said, Still got my freedom.

Where's my son, Uncle Gerald said.

I said, He's gone.

He shook his head. Pierre put his hands around the lady in the jean shorts. She put her head on his shoulder.

You're gone, Uncle Gerald said.

He rolled me to the side. I tried to get up but he put his hands down on my shoulders.

Just like when we used to play, Uncle Gerald said.

I pulled out the pistol and pointed it at his kneecap. Uncle Gerald took a step back. I stood up.

What are you going to do with that, Uncle Gerald said.

The lady in the jean shorts said, Gun.

Pierre said, Son.

Leave us alone, I said.

Pierre said, You shoot.

I nodded my head.

Pierre said, Ma taught you.

She has good aim, I said.

Uncle Gerald moved towards me.

I said, I'll blast you. I said, I'm not Barn or your sister or anything else. I said, I wouldn't care.

You wouldn't, Uncle Gerald said.

I cocked the pistol.

Whoa, Uncle Gerald said.

I said, I'm going back in the house. I said, You all leave now and we won't tell the police and there won't be any trouble. I said, It would be like y'all were never here.

The frogs croaked. The lady in the jean shorts ran her hands through her hair. Pierre scratched his back. Uncle Gerald attacked me. The frogs croaked. He knocked the gun out of my hand and got me to the ground and pinned me.

I said, Fuck.

Pierre picked up the gun. Uncle Gerald rolled me over and picked me up, grabbing onto my shirt. He pushed me away and climbed through window. Pierre gave me the pistol back. He went through the window. The lady in the jean shorts was still standing outside.

I said, After you,

This is none of my business, the lady in the jean shorts said.

I said, It's a lot cooler out here anyway.

I'm glad you're back in your dad's life, the lady in the jean shorts said.

I said, I'm not. I said, He's nowhere near my life. I said, And it's going to stay that way.

He does talk about you and think about you, the lady in the jean shorts said.

I said, He wouldn't have to, if he didn't leave Ma for you.

Yeah, the lady in the jean shorts said.

I went through the window. I could see the flashlights' beams hovering around the hallway walls.

They were all in the living room. There was Ma. There was Pepper. There was Pierre. There was Uncle Gerald. Uncle Gerald was on the floor cursing. Pierre was on the floor shouting in pain.

Fuck, Pierre said.

Uncle Gerald said, Fuck.

Ma laughed.

What is this, Pierre said.

I gave Ma the gun.

Ma said, It's crawfish.

You were always good with crawfish, Pierre said.

They stood up. Ma shot Uncle Gerald in the foot. Uncle Gerald went back to the floor screaming in pain. The crawfish clicked and clacked as he rolled over them. The lady in the jean shorts hurried in, calling Pierre's name.

Not me, Pierre said. Gerald, Pierre said.

Damn it sister, Uncle Gerald said.

Ma said, There's more coming if you don't settle down.

Going back outside, the lady in the jean shorts said. Please don't shoot Pierre, the lady in the jean shorts said.

Ma pointed the gun at Pierre.

Ma said, You got your chicken.

It's not me, Pierre said. Gerald said he needed some help, Pierre said. So I brought him here, Pierre said.

Ma said, Always causing problems.

Uncle Gerald was still rolling on the floor. There was clicking and clacking and crunching.

Bullet, bullet, bullet went the ankle. Claws, claws, claws, went the cracking. Gun, gun, gun went the smoke, and smoke, smoke, smoke went the lips. Hot, hot, hot went the dark. Frog, frog, frog went the throats, and window, window, window went the outside.

Ma flashed the light at Uncle Gerald's foot. The wood was darker around his body.

Sit yourself up, Ma said.

Uncle Gerald stood up on one leg.

Not on the sofa, Ma said.

I got a chair from the kitchen and set it in the living room. Uncle Gerald sat down sticking his hurt leg out.

Can't do much without light, Pepper said.

Ma nodded her head. Pierre spat. Ma cocked the pistol and aimed it at him.

Ma said, You spit one more time in this house I'll shoot your thigh.

Pierre wiped the spit with his shoe.

Ma said, Get some bandages and some rubbing alcohol.

When I got back, Pierre was sitting on the sofa, and Ma was sipping on a beer. Pepper was staring at Uncle Gerald's foot—he was still cursing. Ma slapped him on the back of the head.

Quit that, Ma said. You curse one more time, I'll shoot your mouth, Ma said.

Ma poured the rubbing alcohol on Uncle Gerald's foot, which was resting on the coffee table.

Damn coffee table is getting ruined, Ma said.

Uncle Gerald said, Horse, horse, horse, horse, horse, horse, horse. Uncle Gerald said, Pig, pig, pig, pig, pig, pig, pig, pig, pig. Uncle Gerald said, Shoe, shoe, shoe, shoe, shoe, shoe, shoe, shoe. Uncle Gerald said, Pink, pink, pink, pink, pink, pink, pink, pink. Uncle Gerald said, Ditch, ditch, ditch, ditch, ditch, ditch, ditch, ditch.

Ma wrapped his foot in gauze and then wrapped a towel over the gauze. She used the belt from her robe to secure the towel.

Good as new, Ma said.

Pierre was sitting on the sofa.

Get out of that, Ma said. Ma said, Y'all aren't welcome here.

Pierre stood up and walked up to Uncle Gerald.

Leave now, Ma said.

Not yet, Uncle Gerald said. Uncle Gerald said, I need some money and a place to stay for now. Uncle Gerald said, I need some good rest and sleep.

What's wrong with prison, Ma said. Ma said, They got mattresses.

Uncle Gerald said, I'm not going out. Uncle Gerald said, I'm going to be there for the rest of my life. Uncle Gerald said, I figured I'd escape for a while, until they catch me, and enjoy the free time.

Idiot, Ma said.

Uncle Gerald said, Laurennette.

You got big muscles, Ma said. Ma said, But you got dumber.

Uncle Gerald said, Laurennette.

First thing in the morning, Ma said. Ma said, Y'all out.

Pepper was at the kitchen sink eating an orange. I flashed the light on her. She looked peaceful, like this chaos made her feel at home. She was comfortable.

Get that light out of my face, Pepper said.

She put a slice in my mouth and she kept her finger on my tongue.

Feel the juice, Pepper said.

Her finger left. I chewed. The sweat on my neck felt good. I heard Barn's name, and we walked back to the living room.

No Barn, Ma said.

Uncle Gerald said, Barn.

No Barn, Ma said.

Uncle Gerald said, Barn.

Barn, I said.

Pepper said, Barn.

No Barn, Ma said.

Uncle Gerald said, I owe it to him.

Ma shook her head and puffed smoke.

Uncle Gerald said, One last time before I know there won't be another chance.

Think about him, I said. I said, Gone, gone, gone. I said, Here, here, here.

It's no good, Ma said.

There was a squeak. And there was a squeak. We all turned around. Ma flashed the light and aimed the gun. Uncle Gerald peered over. Pepper and I stood next to each other and looked. Pierre was nodding his head. Ma put the gun behind her back. There was Barn, holding a blanket and a dead snake.

Back to sleep, I said.

He held up the dead snake.

Pepper said, He must have found it in the attic.

I took the dead snake—there was blood, and it was still wet. I shined the light on Barn's hands, and he had blood on his shirt and his hands.

He just killed it, I said.

Ma said, Warrior.

Pierre nodded his head. Uncle Gerald tried to stand up but halfway he went back down on his chair.

Ma said, Shut up.

Back to sleep, I said.

Pepper said, I'll wash him up.

She tapped Barn on the head.

Pepper said, Let's get you cleaned up and sleeping.

Ma said, Light.

Barn rubbed his head against Pepper's knee. He walked up to Uncle Gerald. We all flashed our lights at them. Uncle Gerald stared at Barn. Barn stared back. Barn tapped Uncle Gerald's thigh. Barn tapped Uncle Gerald's shoulder. Barn brushed his shoulder against Uncle Gerald's shoulder, and Barn looked at his father's wounded foot. He took off his shirt and gave it to Uncle Gerald. He put the blanket on top of Uncle Gerald's foot. Barn walked circles around Uncle Gerald, and the crawfish slid across the room, making clacks and clicks and zips.

I've done great wrong, Uncle Gerald said.

Barn kept walking in circles.

All of this was worth it, Uncle Gerald said.

He lifted his arms like he was going to pick Barn up and set him on his lap, but he put them back down and bowed his head.

See, Ma said.

Pepper put her arm around my shoulders. Barn picked up a crawfish and tried to peel it.

You brushed your teeth, Ma said. Ma said, We'll have some more later.

Barn put the crawfish on top of his father's head. Uncle Gerald took it and held it up to the flashlights.

A fine crawfish, Uncle Gerald said.

The sirens came.

Ma said, It wasn't me.

I know, Uncle Gerald said.

There was screeching, and barking, and there were the frogs—stubborn and croaking.

Pierre helped Uncle Gerald up.

It was good seeing you, Uncle Gerald said.

Ma tapped him on the shoulder.

Pierre said, Same here.

Ma told him to shut up. Me and Pepper took the boards down from the door, opened the door, and broke through the boards on the other side. Ma had done a pretty good job of making sure they were secure when she was putting them up. Hot air met hot air. With Pierre's help, Uncle Gerald limped towards the front. Through the doorway, underneath the streetlight, there was the lady in the jean shorts. There was red and blue and yellow and there were officers pointing their guns at us. Barn put his hands up. We all put our hands up.

You got a license for that gun, I said.

Ma said, Sure do.

Self-defense, Pierre said.

Uncle Gerald said, It'll all be okay.

We all walked outside. The officers knew what to do. We were questioned while the bubblegum lights whirled around the houses of the neighborhood, making everything look tasty. Barn liked it as he moved his head around in circles along with the twirling light. It was all a circus.

I said, It's all a circus.

Uncle Gerald was cuffed. As he was helped into the back seat he looked at me.

Tell Barn not to look, Uncle Gerald said.

Barn looked.

I said, Don't look.

Uncle Gerald looked at me with watery eyes.

Tell Barn, Uncle Gerald. Uncle Gerald said, Tell Barn that I wish that if—that if.

The car door shut. He rested his head against the window. Barn waved. Uncle Gerald didn't look.

Ma said, Idiot.

The lady in the jean shorts held Pierre's hand. Pierre asked if they could get a ride to the nearest bus stop.

Ma said, Walk it.

Pepper was in a robe. And then the neighborhood was empty and dark and quiet. Barn stood at the edge of the driveway watching his dad go away. Once the car was out of sight, Barn waved again.

I said, Fruity Pebbles.

Me and Pepper, we were at the lake. It wasn't too deep—standing straight, the water would come up to about our chins. The lakebed felt slimy and gritty and good. Pepper was swimming. She was a strong swimmer. When her arms and head would pop up from the water after each stroke, I could see her muscles flexed and tight. I wasn't too much of a swimmer. I liked to wade, and I waded and watched Pepper swim.

After she was done, she floated around on her back. I went up to her. Her chest was speckled with drops and I ran my fingers around her nipples. She didn't say anything. She just kept floating around on her back from bank to bank. The ducks weren't too scared of us. They didn't take off and scurry away, they just stood on the banks and quacked and waddled around. I brought some bread for them so that helped ease any kind of tension.

Barn, Pepper said. We should bring Barn next time, Pepper said.

I dunked my head and listened to the gushing water. I could never open my eyes underwater, though, but the sound itself was worth it. I came back up and the hot air felt good.

I said, The ducks will take him.

The ducks would like him, Pepper said.

Barn would like the ducks, I said.

I swam up to her and kissed her belly button. She stuck her hand in the water and grabbed me and pulled me in closer.

We are aqua, Pepper said.

I said, Lake menders.

Pepper dived under and didn't come up for thirty seconds. I dived under and didn't come up for thirty seconds. We both dived under and didn't come up for thirty seconds. She took my arm and pulled me towards the bank, where there were some roots growing over. I looked up and saw a hawk going over us, and I looked around and saw nothing else. I looked around and there was a redbird on a branch. I pointed at it and Pepper looked up.

Feisty, Pepper said.

She stood up on the bank and rolled around in the mud. She stood up on the bank and covered herself in fallen leaves and dirt and twigs.

Cover me, Pepper said.

She got down, and I covered her even more, and she looked like she was in earth. I saw her hand move closer to her body as some of leaves and twigs moved away. There was a quack and a flutter of wings. Pepper closed her eyes and her hand was moving fast up and down. She got up and straddled a root that was growing out from the ground and over the lake, and she moved back and forth and moaned and closed her eyes and opened them. I went back into the lake and watched her with my hands under the water. When she was done and I was done we lay on the bank and looked through the branches and saw bits and pieces of sky and cloud.

Good bark, Pepper said.

I WAS MUTTY

I was Mutty. I was a prince of nothing with empty hands and hardened palms. When no one was around, I was a palace—I was a castle full of rocks and tin and flattened tires.

I was Mutty. And there was nothing. My tattered robe—torn and dragging against the spiky ground—no longer had shape. My body had sunken. My chin, scarred and blue, dented as the air pushed against it.

What were your hands? What did your elbows say? Where were your eyes? My knees shuddered at the thought of everything, and when the clouds teased, I lifted my arms and waited for the drops.

I was Mutty. Filled with nothing, I walked from one side of the world to the other with an echoing head, repeating everything, every step reminding me that this earth was a clump of clay and mud and cow.

Tickling dew. Heavy air. I was starving. Empty plates and scrape, scrape, scrape—the screeching and scratching bounced against the walls of what I was. Who was I? Nothing was best when everyone was around, and round, round, round went the world. I was Mutty, and I stood still.

What happened when morning collided with night? What happened when clocks met miles? What happened when the evening looked sad?

Sunlight and the sun, they reflected. The windows were glossy. The glass was speckled with pollen. My hair was singed with sunlight, and the sunlight bent this way and that, to make the day look broken.

I was Mutty. I was broken, and I broke. If only we were all smiling. If only we were all good. If only our hands were always together, clasped and strong and ready for the chains that try to pull them apart—these chains that keep the fallen gates together. These chains that keep the choppy fences slanted, they are stubborn and angry. Let us go away. Let us be here. Go away, and let us go there.

TRUCK

Me and Pepper were in the truck and after the rain had stopped, we went out into the field. The truck did good. The tires spun with an attitude. The mud itself had its own attitude. Pepper was good with the gears, and kept the windows down so that everything outside would come inside. It stung when the bits and pieces of muck hit my forehead or my closed eyes or my nose. Pepper was laughing.

The grinding sounded like Ma's snoring, and as Pepper backed up and went forward and backed up and went forward, the engine would change tones, just like when Ma would turn over to the other side. The front window was a wall of dripping brown earth, endless, as it moved down to the hood of the truck. Pepper was naked, but the mud covered her skin. It dripped between her breasts, it blended in with her nipples, and it caressed her thighs. Pepper stopped laughing. She was panting. As the truck fought the field, grunting and grumbling and roaring, like an angry horse, Pepper was getting more and more excited.

The truck got stuck. Pepper shifted gears and pushed down. She let go and pushed down. She shifted gears. It reminded me of when I took Barn to go fishing and we got caught near the banks over some sunken roots. Like then, we were floating and trapped, and the truck rocked back and forth trying to find a way out. Pepper's back rubbed against the seat and her legs were going up and down. Her hands were dark and wet and she closed her eyes as the truck spat and breathed in and out. The mud kept coming in, making the inside look like one big chocolate shake.

Pepper said, Get out.

She leaned over and pulled the handle and opened the door.

Pepper said, I want to suck you.

I got out.

Pepper said, Take off your clothes.

I pulled my shirt off, sticky and heavy. I had to roll it off my body bit by bit. There was rain. The truck was still running. It sat there, shaking.

You did good, I said.

Pepper cupped a handful of mud and rubbed it against her sides. She wiped her breasts and went to the ground, almost camouflaged, blended in with the soaked earth.

72

This is the world, Pepper said.

She kicked the back of my legs and I went down on my knees. She put her hand around me. She rubbed her face against me. She covered my legs and my stomach with mud, and spat on me to clean me up. I closed my eyes and lifted my head. I closed my eyes and felt the rain coming down. I closed my eyes and felt the air around me fade. Me and Pepper, we faded with the air. I closed my eyes and everything was spinning.

Fuck, Pepper said.

I got down. She got on her knees and hands. When I was behind her, she didn't look back at me.

When I was on top of her, her hands were grappling, scratching, smoothing out the mud. Her eyes were looking past me.

Can you see inside my head, I said.

Pepper said, I can see the other side.

What do you see, I said.

Pepper said, I see a mad sky.

She was on top of me. She wasn't moving her whole body, just a small movement of her hips.

I said, Easy.

Today the earth needs comforting, Pepper said.

And she sped up. And she was bouncing. And was pushing me against the ground. I was far in, almost buried in this drenched earth. Pepper was lost. She was gone now. She pulled her own hair. She pulled my hair. She screamed and mumbled and then it was all quiet.

I said, Who am I.

Who are you, Pepper said.

She licked her lips and she looked all around.

Truck, Pepper said.

She looked at the sky. She rubbed the back of her neck with her muddy hands and turned towards me.

Do I know you, Pepper said.

BARN WAS SICK AND BARN WAS TAKING CARE OF ME

Spat, spat, spat went the spit. Throat, throat, throat went the scratch. Lungs, lungs, lungs went the cough. Cough, cough, cough went the phlegm, and chin, chin, chin went the drip. Soup, soup, soup went the sip. Sharp, sharp, sharp went the lemon, and hands, hands, hands went the melt. Roof, roof, roof went the shard. Legs, legs, legs went the cross. Sky, sky, sky went the sun. Back, back, back went the red. Wrist, wrist, wrist went the pulse. Nose, nose, nose went the chimney. Rock, rock, rock went the forth. Eyes, eyes, eyes went the closed. Sweet, sweet, sweet went the lips. Buds, buds, buds went the tongue and wheeze, wheeze, wheeze went the ribs.

Barn was bad off. His forehead was hot and damp, and his chest was hurting. The coughing went for twenty seconds at a time—these spasms made me want to pull out his lungs and set them in the dishwasher. He was staying tough, though, but his frustration at not being able to do jumping jacks or cartwheels or frog jumps got the best of him. His eyes would turn red and water but he kept the tears from coming out. There was much to learn from Barn—even when he was in his weakest state. He tried to go out and play in the field or in the barn, but Ma kept him close.

Hay fever, Ma said.

Barn tugged on her muumuu.

Mad cow disease, Ma said.

Barn tilted his head.

Soup, Ma said.

Barn scratched at her thigh. After he finished the lemon-pepper soup—Ma had made it really bitter and sharp—and after he finished scrunching up his face, Barn darted outside.

Rough soup, I said.

Ma said, I know. Ma said, It was bad.

Good for him, I said.

Ma said, Go get him.

I was hoping that with the cough and the hurting, Barn would somehow start talking—whether by accident or on purpose—but the coughs were the only things that came out of his throat.

He was on the roof again. I heard the coughing through the chimney.

I said, Ma.

Ma said, Up.

She gave me a bottle of medicine and a thermos full of chocolate.

Ma said, Make sure he still has his nose.

Nose, I said.

Ma said, Look for it right below his eyes. Ma said, Somewhere in the middle of his face.

Eyes, I said.

Ma sat in the recliner and stared at the wall.

Up on the roof, Barn sat cross-legged, beating his fists against his chest.

I said, Loosen it up.

I patted him on the back. He put his hand on my forehead. Then he put the back of his hand against my neck, just underneath the side of my face. His hand was hot and sweaty.

I said, I'm fine.

He took my hand and flipped it to where the palm was facing the sky and gently put his fingers on my wrist.

I said, Are you taking care of me.

Barn pushed his fingers against my stomach.

I said, Intestines.

Barn patted me on the back and stood up.

I said, Am I going to be okay.

Barn coughed. He stumbled back into sitting cross-legged. I gave him his medicine, and he spat it out. I gave it to him again, and he spat it out.

I said, It'll help.

Ma shouted through the chimney.

Ma said, Nose.

I said, It's still there.

Ma said, Cauliflower and oranges.

In a bit, I said.

Barn coughed for a long time. I could only watch him struggle as he breathed in hard for air. He spat phlegm—the glob made a thick sound as it hit the shard. He was wheezing, sounding like a dying cow taking its last breath of life, and his shirt was drenched. I took it off of him and rolled it up and wrung out the sweat.

I said, Bacteria.

He took off his shorts. His body was red and throbbing, and I wished that I was inside his rib cage.

I said, I'll keep you going.

Barn lifted his hand and looked at the sky with his mouth open. He closed his eyes and rocked his body back and forth—the sweat poured down from the side of his face and onto his chest. The shards around him were dark and wet. He breathed in and out, wheezing and coughing until it went away for a bit. I gave him his medicine and he spat it out. I gave it to him again and he swallowed. The chocolate still hadn't melted yet, and I pulled out a few pieces and gave it to him. His eyes were wide and round—his tongue stuck out of his mouth a bit. Before taking a bite, he paused and looked at the roof, and he stretched out his arms, offering the chocolate to me.

I said, They're for you.

He put one in his mouth and sighed.

I said, I love you Barn.

AT THE XXX

We were at the XXX shop looking at XXX things. The store was colorful, pinks and greens and blues and reds everywhere. There was a tiny lady behind the counter—she must have weighed about 90 pounds.

Pepper said, I'd crush her.

There was one other person there—a huge man who must have weighed around 400 pounds. He was checking out at the counter—there was a beep after a beep after a beep after a beep.

He must have found some things, I said.

Pepper walked to a glass case full of dildos. Another couple walked in—two muscular people, one was a guy, and the other was a lady. The lady had blonde hair and was looking this way. The man did, too. She had on a mini-skirt and a tight white t-shirt. She was wearing a black bra underneath. The guy was in jeans and a tank top. His arms were covered in tattoos of spikes and wires.

Let's get some tattoos someday, I said.

Pepper said, We will.

She looked at the blonde haired girl.

Pepper said, You like that girl.

She's pretty, I said.

Pepper said, Maybe she can join us.

I looked at a penis pump.

Pepper said, Maybe that guy can join us, too.

I looked at the guy again.

There'd be no place for me, I said.

Pepper said, You got to fight for your place.

Do I need a penis pump, I said.

She patted me on the back. She tried to open the glass display case but it was locked.

Dildos are stolen a lot, I said.

The tiny lady behind the counter asked us if we needed help.

I said, Maybe she can join us, too.

I'd crush her, Pepper said.

The tiny lady walked up to us and unlocked the glass case. Pepper picked up a small box containing a pink vibrating dildo. She opened it up and took it out.

Feels good, Pepper said.

She put it between her legs. I looked at this huge machine. It was a masturbator for guys.

I said, Scary.

It had a photo of a guy who looked a lot like the guy who had just walked into the store.

XXX, Pepper said.

She put the dildo back in the box and moved on to the next display case.

Find yourself something, Pepper said.

I said, You're good.

I know, Pepper said.

She ran her fingers across a whip.

But let's make this an adventure, Pepper said.

She handed me the whip. The tiny lady asked us if we needed any help again.

You want a good night, Pepper said.

The tiny lady ran her fingers through her long brown hair and twisted it around her index finger. Her shirt was cut short, ending above her belly button.

The tiny lady said, Got plans tonight.

I'd crush you, Pepper said.

The tiny lady said, Come back or come get me.

She gave Pepper receipt paper with her number on it.

The tiny lady said, We'll put that whip to use.

She walked back to the counter.

She'd crush you, Pepper said.

XXX went the red. XXX went the blue. XXX went the yellow. XXX went the green. XXX went the purple. XXX went the orange, and XXX went the pink. Do, do, do went the dil. Pump, pump, pump went the big. Whip, whip, whip went the lash. Face, face, face went the mask. Leather, leather, leather went the thong. Zzzz, zzzz, zzzz went the vibrate. Style, style, style went the doggy and wet, wet, wet went the ring.

Pepper looked at the vibrators and picked up pocket-sized one. I picked up some edible underwear.

I said, For Barn.

It was strawberry flavored.

I want to try one, Pepper said. She said, I'm kind of hungry.

I picked up another one. And I picked up another one for myself—vanilla flavored. The other couple was looking at some items around where we were standing. The blonde haired lady smiled at me. I nodded my head.

What's good, the blonde haired lady said.

I said, Vibrators.

Whips, Pepper said.

The blonde haired lady looked at the muscle guy.

I'm up for anything, the muscle guy said.

The blonde haired lady said, It's our first time here.

It's a circus, Pepper said.

I said, Colorful.

Come join us this weekend, Pepper said.

The muscle guy looked at Pepper. He looked her up and down and he looked at her legs. He moved his eyes up and stopped at her hips. The blonde haired lady looked at Pepper, too—she was looking at her chest. I was looking at the blonde haired lady's chest. She looked at me looking at her. I was picturing her in her underwear—with her black bra. I pictured her and Pepper kissing and running their hands across each other's bodies—breasts, nipples, tongues, and there was moaning and wetness and skin on skin, and there were legs here and there. They were on top of each other and their fingers were inside of each other, and there was licking and panting. I was bulging. The blonde haired lady looked at my bulge. The muscle guy and the blonde haired lady didn't say anything to each other—it was a silent agreement.

The blonde haired lady said, We're up for it.

Good, Pepper said.

The blonde haired lady's nipples were sticking out—hard and frozen. Pepper had her hand on my lower back. We exchanged phone numbers. They ended up leaving without buying anything. They must have been so nervous or so excited about the arrangement, that it took the place of buying a vibrator or a penis pump or watermelon scented lube.

Handcuffs, Pepper said.

They were fluffy and blue. There was The Dirty Man—in plain and boots. The Dirty Man was there with his scratchy skin and red-tanned body. He walked straight to us, a toothpick in his mouth. His hands were bandaged.

It could have been a nice night, I said.

Pepper said, Fuck.

The Dirty Man rubbed his belly.

What's up brah, The Dirty Man said.

He stuck out his hand. Pepper's arm was around mine. We walked way. The Dirty Man didn't like this.

Respect, The Dirty Man said.

He grabbed my shoulder and turned me around. The tiny lady

shouted at us. Pepper's arm was still around mine.

You talk to me when I talk to you, The Dirty Man said.

The tiny lady said, My brother is a cop.

You shake my hand when I stick my hand out, The Dirty Man said.

He stuck out his hand. I didn't shake it.

Pepper, The Dirty Man said.

I put the handcuffs, and the edible underwear, and the whip, and the lube, and the dildo, and the vibrator on the counter.

You look at me Pepper, The Dirty Man said.

The Dirty Man put his hand on her face and squeezed her cheeks while lifting her chin up. I pushed it off.

You look at me Pepper, The Dirty Man said.

Pepper kept looking to the side.

You're mine, The Dirty Man said.

I said, Fuck.

I hit him in the face. He didn't go down though and pushed me over the counter. Pepper shouted. The tiny lady shouted. The Dirty Man was on top of me. He kept slapping me in the face. His knees dug into my stomach.

Hand, hand, hand went the smack. Smack, smack, smack went the slap. Face, face, face went the palm. Teeth, teeth, teeth went the grit.

He got up and jumped back over the counter and went to Pepper.

I'll be seeing you, The Dirty Man said.

Pepper said, I'm not yours.

You're all mine, The Dirty Man said.

Pepper said, One day I'll kill you.

Only after I get you real good, The Dirty Man said.

I pushed him in the back.

Bring your toys, The Dirty Man said.

The Dirty Man winked. He walked out. We apologized to the tiny lady and helped her clean up. After we bought what we wanted we made our way out of the store.

Don't forget to give me a call sometime, the tiny lady said.

Pepper said, Keep your legs open.

Whip, whip, whip went the leather.

And the bulls shuffled their hooves and jerked their heads. There were jeans and boots and hats and ropes. And the bulls looked mad. Mad, mad, mad bulls and their dreams of freedom. They were made to throw us off their backs. They were made with angry eyes. They were made to snort and kick the dirt.

There was a strong smell of manure and dirt, and everything around us was thick and heavy.

Pepper looked on with a sad face.

It's not fair, Pepper said.

I said, Their anger fuels them.

They should be gone, Pepper said.

It didn't take her long to get into it. Pepper was real competitive and once she saw the first few rides not lasting longer than a couple of seconds, she wanted to give it a try.

Twelve seconds, Pepper said.

I said, You wish.

She looked at me.

I could last twelve seconds on any bull, Pepper said.

I said, I could only last four seconds with you.

Not even, Pepper said.

The next bull was Cap. He was in the stall, and the cowboy was wrapping himself in rope and tied himself to the bull. He was wearing black jeans and a black hat and a black shirt. The crowd cheered when he got into the stall and onto the bull. They were all shouting his name.

It took him a while to get himself set on the bull. Cap wasn't gentle in the stall. There was snorting and shuffling around and jerks, and the rider had to untie himself and get off the bull and get back onto the bull and re-tie himself.

The arena was dirt, and there were these barrels all around the place and there were bales of hay. The bell sounded. The stall unlocked. Cap came out and the crowd started yelling.

One second.

Two seconds.

Three Seconds.

Pepper moaned.

Five seconds.

Pepper clasped her hands.

Seven seconds.

The bull was empty and the rider was in the dirt. He kept rolling and rolling and as soon as the bull was empty, there were clowns. They started to dance around Cap, and the bull went this way and that.

Get them, Pepper said. Pepper said, Hit them.

She was rooting for Cap. She was always rooting for the bull. The bull was what Pepper knew.

I said, Toro.

The cowboy stood up and looked at the bull for a second before running to the side and jumping over the wall. He rubbed the side of his body and fixed his collar. The dirt in the arena had these trails and paths and we could tell where the bulls had been and where the riders had fallen.

Pepper was standing and clapping her hands, yelling the bull's name over and over again. The clowns were dancing, and the bull caught one of them in the back of the thigh. The clown flew in the air for a second and landed on his back. Another clown ran in front of Cap and another clown threw a rope around the bull and it caught around its neck. The crowd oooooed. Pepper started cursing.

Break it, Pepper said.

They led the bull back into the stall, where it quietly stood as if nothing had happened. It was over and there was just a humming of voices. Two clowns helped the fallen clown get up and they helped him limp out of the arena. The crowd clapped their hands and cheered the clowns as they got out.

The bull won, Pepper said.

Her nipples were hard. The bull had made her hard. The dirt had made her hard. The clowns had made her mad. Her thighs were tense and flexed.

The next bull was Ace Kicker. Ace Kicker was more gentle in the stall than Cap. It didn't take long for the next rider to tie himself up on the bull. There was popcorn and butter and hot dogs and beer.

When I looked around the stands, I saw endless heads—they were all talking and smiling and shouting and laughing. This was the rodeo, and the bulls were winning, and the fans were still happy because there was plenty to see.

When the stall unlocked, I sneezed, and the rider was in the dirt, and the bull was empty. Before the clowns could jump out of the barrels, Ace Kicker was all over the cowboy, and there were legs and arms in the air. The clowns finally got out and they got the bull back into the stall, and it was all quiet. The rider didn't move.

Pepper was smiling.

She said, Kicker.

There was a team of hospital people and they came out with a stretcher and they took about ten minutes to get the rider onto the stretcher. Everyone was clapping. The rider stuck out his hand and waved and gave a thumbs up, and the clapping and cheering got louder.

What are they cheering for, Pepper said.

I said, Alive.

What about the bull, Pepper said.

I looked at the stall, and the bull was facing the other way. Its head was down and gently moved back and forward and it shuffled its hooves.

I said, It'll be good.

That's a good bull, Pepper said.

I said, You wouldn't last a second.

Pepper was still confident.

I'm good with bulls, Pepper said.

She stuck her hand in a bag of popcorn and started chewing. We watched the next bull, and the next bull, and the next bull. We watched all the bulls for two something hours and no one lasted longer than seven seconds, and Pepper was happy.

Good for the bulls, Pepper said.

She was drunk by then, and she was ready to go. We walked past the stalls and Pepper stopped and looked at one of them. The bull went up to Pepper, and Pepper ran her fingers between its eyes.

Stay strong, Pepper said.

The bull was gentle and nodded its head. Maybe Pepper could have lasted twelve seconds.

The tiny lady was at the door. She was wearing a short white dress, holding three bottles of malt liquor. The clothing was thin, thin, thin, and her pink, pink, pink underwear was hinting.

Pepper said, Come in.

The tiny lady was wearing some kind of body scent lotion. She walked in, moving her hips side to side. I looked at Pepper. Pepper was looking at her.

Thanks for calling, the tiny lady said.

The tiny lady stuck her tongue in Pepper's mouth. Pepper's hands were around the tiny lady's waist. I was standing there watching them. I was bulging. They stopped.

The tiny lady gave Pepper a bottle. She came up to me and grabbed me and licked my chin. She gave me a bottle.

The tiny lady said, Drink up.

Pepper was guzzling it down. I was taking sips out of mine. The tiny lady had already finished her bottle. She sat on the couch, next to Pepper—her legs opened, revealing pink. She rubbed her hands on Pepper's thighs, who was wearing blue lingerie. Together, they looked like cotton candy.

Shouldn't we talk first, I said.

The tiny lady said, Let's fuck.

That was a good conversation, Pepper said.

They opened their mouths at each other. Their hands were on themselves and they were on each other. The tiny lady was keeping Pepper's attention. She wasn't backing down. Pepper liked it. Pepper moaned. The tiny lady moaned. I stared.

The tiny lady said, Come sit.

I sat on the coffee table, facing them.

The tiny lady said, Come sit.

Come sit, Pepper said.

I was surrounded by thongs. There were only two, but it felt like a hundred. A hundred thongs. Their hands were on my lap, rubbing me back and forth, grabbing my bulge while they touch the tips of each other's tongues with their own. Taste buds. The tiny lady put her head against my neck and breathed hard and whispered.

We are all hard, the tiny lady said.

Pepper got up and straddled me and moved her hips back and

forth. The tiny lady stood up on the back of the couch and Pepper licked her as the tiny lady pulled up her white dress.

Pepper said, Like mud.

The tiny lady's tiny hands were on top of Pepper's head guiding her to thighs. I stuck my fingers in Pepper's mouth. I stuck my fingers in the tiny lady. Pepper stuck herself inside of me. Pepper stuck her tongue in the tiny lady. The tiny lady stuck her fingers inside herself. The tiny lady grabbed my bulge. We were all everywhere, and the ceiling fan hummed.

Hum, hum, hum went the fan. Twirl, twirl, twirl went the ceiling. Legs, legs, legs went the open. Tongue, tongue, tongue went the triangles. Nails, nails, nails went the neck. Three, three, three went the one, and one, one, one went the three. Up, up, up went the side, and down, down, down, went the world.

In between the smacking and the clapping, there was moaning and soothing. The tiny lady's eyes were glossy. Pepper's eyes were gone. I shifted this way and that to make the shapes fit—to make the sweat fall in place.

Toes, toes, toes went the mouth. Lick, lick, lick went the wet. Stone, stone, stone went the nipples. Skin, skin, skin, went the three.

Pepper took breaks and watched. The tiny lady took breaks and watched. I took breaks and watched. Sometimes, I thought about Barn. I wished that he could fly away from it all—fly away from the top of the roof and leave us all behind. He belonged in another world.

We all took breaks and breathed.

Barn was standing in the front yard eating edible underwear.
There were clouds. In between the clouds, there were sunbeams.
Barn was shiny in it all. His belly poked out, and his skin was
glittery. One eye was closed—his head tilted slightly. He munched.
The cicadas were humming, loud and free. A grasshopper caught
Barn's attention. He trailed it, as it hopped in between the bits of
grass. He stopped and looked up at the sky again—one eye closed.

I said, Don't go.

Barn didn't look at me.

I said, Don't leave.

I pictured him leaving the yard, upwards, towards the space
between the clouds. He was going fast—he was just a blur. In the
yard, he looked sturdy and confident, like if he really wanted to, at
that moment, he could fly away, even without a cape.

Ma opened the door, which was still covered in pieces of
splintered wooden boards from the storm. She was holding a
wooden stirring spoon.

Corn maque choux, Ma said.

I said, The air smells good.

Come get it, Ma said.

I said, Barn.

Potassium, Ma said.

Barn didn't turn around. He kept looking up.

I said, What are you thinking about.

Barn's belly poked out from under his shirt. He finished
chewing the edible underwear and wiped his hands on the grass.
He stretched his arms and legs and moved his hips in a circular
motion like he was doing aerobics.

I said, Corn maque choux.

His feet, bare and dirty, rubbed against the yard.

I said, Bull.

He took a few steps back—as close to the house as possible.

I said, Don't go Barn. I said, Please stay.

He took off. He sprinted across the yard and then made a loop
around the mailbox and made his way back into the house.

I said, Potassium.

I stayed out on the front yard and looked up, like Barn, and
crouched down and jumped up. I didn't get too high. I tried again.

I tried again and again and again.

I said, Gravity.

Barn could have broken that force during that moment he was staring up into the sky. He just didn't want to.

I said, Not yet at least.

The Dirty Man was in the parking lot of the gas station. He was standing at the side of the building, where there wasn't any light. I could see his cowboy hat. I went inside to get Barn a Rain Crunch Chocolate and Vanilla Cookie. Ma wanted a slushie, too, and I was craving some sunflower seeds. It was night out—late into the night, on a Sunday night. There was another guy inside the store besides the employee. He looked bad. Red eyes and stumbling. He was mumbling in front of the beer fridge, opening and closing the door and bumping into everything around him. The guy working at the counter kept looking at him. I was checking out.

I said, He's off.

I got my gun, the employee said.

I said, This'll be all.

He scanned everything, while the guy at the back was still making a ruckus.

You quiet down, the employee said. Or you'll leave, the employee said.

The mumbling man kept mumbling. He took out two cases of beer and walked into a stand of beef jerky, knocking it over.

No service, the employee said.

The mumbling man said, Beer.

Get out, the employee said.

The mumbling man said, Beer.

The employee left the counter and walked up to him.

You pick all that up, the employee said.

The mumbling man spat on the floor. There was some dribble on the side of his lip. There was mucus just under his nose.

Disgusting, the employee said.

I sipped a bit out of Ma's slushie and started chewing some seeds.

The employee grabbed the mumbling man by the arm, but the mumbling man pushed him away. The mumbling man stumbled backwards, hitting his back against the beer fridge door.

I'm calling the cops, the employee said.

The mumbling man said, Wait.

He looked at me and stared at me and looked at me. I tried not to stare back, but I couldn't look anywhere else, and I didn't want to leave the employee by himself.

Fuck, I said.

The Dirty Man walked in.

The Dirty Man said, Fancy this.

He took off his hat and ran his fingers across its brim. His skin was dark pink, and his eyes were red.

Breath, breath, breath went the stink.

The Dirty Man said, Well, well, well.

He got up close to me. I took a step back. I should have gotten Pepper some string cheese.

The Dirty Man said, What you got there.

The mumbling man continued to make a mess. The employee walked towards the counter and picked up the phone.

The Dirty Man said, Hold on now.

He looked at the mumbling man.

The Dirty Man said, Come on. The Dirty Man said, Let's go.

Beer, the mumbling man said.

The Dirty Man said, We got some at the place.

The mumbling man started cackling. He walked towards The Dirty Man, pushing against my shoulder.

The Dirty Man said, I'll be seeing you.

You should brush your teeth, I said.

The Dirty Man laughed.

They're yellow, I said.

The Dirty Man ran his tongue against his teeth.

The Dirty Man said, Tastes good. The Dirty Man said, Enjoy your slushie now.

The Dirty Man opened the door and pushed the mumbling man out before following him.

The employee said, Rascals.

I helped him clean up the mess and put the beef jerky back on the stand. I remembered to pick up some string cheese for Pepper. The employee let me have it for free because of the help. I had almost finished Ma's slushie. There was beer at home though.

Outside, in the parking lot, all of the lights had gone out, and the whole place was dark. There weren't any cars on the road. I could smell a dead armadillo. There were some crickets, too. I went over to Ma's car to fill it up before going back home.

Gas, gas, gas went the glunk. Car, car, car went the thump. Dark, dark, dark went the humid.

It was filled up halfway, about seven gallons, when there was some thumping coming from the side of the gas station. The Dirty

Man and the mumbling man were shouting at each other and kicking the bumper of a van. I turned back around and saw a face and a wooden board. I saw the tires of Ma's car and some shoes. I saw the ground. I heard footsteps.

Kick, kick, kick went the ribs. Head, head, head went the sting. Scrape, scrape, scrape went the ground. Skin, skin, skin, went the gas. Shout, shout, shout went the voice. Board, board, board went the back. Grunt, grunt, grunt went the mouth. Chin, chin, chin went the cement.

I tried to get back up.

Curl, curl, curl went the body. Body, body, body went the beat.

You fuck, said the voice.

Fuckin' little fuck, said the voice.

Always getting' in the fuckin' way, said the voice.

You fuck, said the voice.

Thanks for the help with the beef jerky, said the voice.

Pepper is going to get it bad, said the voice.

At least you got some free string cheese, said the voice.

I tried to get back up. All I saw were boots and tires. Burn, burn, burn went the face. The cement was rough against my skin. I thought about Barn. He'll be okay. He'll take care of Ma. Don't fly away, Barn. Take Ma with you, Barn. He would have liked the Rain Crunch Chocolate and Vanilla Cookie—I had been meaning to get it for him for the longest time. Ma's slushie was no longer though. I should have gotten her another one. String cheese.

Pepper is going to get fucked real good, said the voice.

The cement was red and wet. The shoes were shiny.

I said, Fuck.

It was getting darker. I closed my eyes. It got darker. The voices were there. I could still see the boots—they were flashing bright in my head. It was getting darker.

ROPE AND CHAIR

There was pain, and it was dark, and my eyes were open. I couldn't see anything. I could feel my eyelashes against cloth. The rope around my wrists was tight. It burned. My legs were tied, too. There was pain. My ribs were there. I tried to twist but there was no movement. I kept moving my head as if that would help me to see my surroundings. I closed my eyes.

There was dripping. Kitchen?

The cloth tickled my nose. I sneezed. I wasn't blind. Sore neck. Sore stomach. Sore head. Sore back. There was pain.

Drip, drip, drip went the head. There were squeaking doors and footsteps. There were voices. Muffled. There was a bit of light coming from underneath the cloth. The ropes burned.

Tight, tight, tight, went the friction. Twist, twist, twist went the world. Dark, dark, dark, went the light. Ribs, ribs, ribs, went the bruise. There was my head, and it was ringing.

Bell, bell, bell went the ears. Buzz, buzz, buzz went the brain. Crack, crack, crack went the knees. Joints, joints, joints went the swelling. Ding, ding, ding went the bell. The frequency was low and numbing.

HORSE THE COW

Horse wasn't doing too healthy the last time she was chewing grass. Her udders were dirty and she was moving around slow. She had been with us since Barn moved in with us, and she was Barn's favorite cow, too. I was hoping that I would be able to see her one last time if I could get out of this darkness. Ma would give her a good burial. Horse had done good for us. Good milk. Good chewing. Good eyes. She would come up to Barn like a dog, waiting to be stroked, waiting to be petted. Barn would ride her sometimes too and he would sleep next to her when Horse wanted to get some shade under the oak. Horse the cow—she had done good for us.

I wondered what Ma was thinking. I pictured her in the recliner, chain smoking and calling out vegetables. She was probably halfway through a case of beer, too. Ma was such a good ma. For both Barn and me—she taught us the good ways. Barn was on the right track—all because of Ma. Pepper had been good for both of them. She was someone different that Ma could talk to—Ma didn't have too many friends. I knew she was lonely, but she never tried to make any changes. She was also someone Ma could talk about, with me—sparking some curiosity, hoping that one day we would get married.

You're going to marry her, Ma said.

I said, If she says yes.

She's a good girl, Ma said.

I said, She's got a glimpse into something we can't see.

Like Barn, Ma said.

I said, They both got something in their blood.

She takes her clothes off a lot, Ma said.

I said, They're special.

Pepper was probably naked as I was sitting all tied up. Pepper. They wanted to get to her. She better know to get away. She better know to protect herself. She better shoot that gun.

The Dirty Man. The Dirty Man and the mumbling man. And there was one more guy, too. The one who started kicking me. Three fools. Pepper was waiting for her chance. She would get her turn to get back at The Dirty Man. Let them get to her. Three fools. Let them get to her. The Three Fucks. The three pieces of litter. The three idiots. I should get Ma on them, too. She would

92

handle them all in one go, just like she did with Pierre and Uncle Gerald. Ma wasn't scared of anything. I had never seen Ma being scared of anything. Ma and Pepper—the superheroes. The Two Forces of Light. And Barn would be their sidekick, and when he got old enough his strength would be so grand, he could fly from here to the end of the universe within a second. The three fools. The Three Forces Of Light.

Ribs. I kept on trying to turn my head like it would somehow automatically help me to see again. The dripping was still there. The voices were gone though. The doors weren't squeaking anymore. There weren't any footsteps. I closed my eyes.

Pepper would have this look in her eyes, when the sun was coming down and when we were in the field, where her eyes could just engulf everything. She was something special. Whether we made it through together or not, Pepper had something that no one else had. Sometimes, I would ask her, too.

What do you have, I said.

Pepper said, Nothing.

In your eyes, I said. I said, What do you have in your eyes.

Pepper said, I can't see my eyes. Pepper said, I got nothing.

You got the clouds in your eyes, I said. I said, the sun, and the earth and the meteors.

Pepper said, Shut the fuck up.

There's this light in you when you're like this, I said.

Pepper said, I got pollen in my eyes.

And then she would go running across the field and shout until her lungs had tired. And sometimes when she wasn't looking, I would look at her when she would be feeding the goats, through the barn window, and I could hear her singing these farm songs about hay and chickens, and her voice sounded like she had the world inside of her. This was during her good days, when she didn't have anything to worry about. All of the animals were quiet—the cows, the horses, the chickens and pigs, and the goats—they all stayed quiet and listened to her sing.

Singing Pepper. Pepper, sing. I wanted to hear her sing again.

Let them get to Pepper. I just wanted to be there to see her wrath. And then she could sing freely again.

The door squeaked. Wood, wood, wood, went the floor, and wood, wood, wood, went the thump. No voice. There was a kick. The world felt horizontal. One side of my body was against the floor. The other side of my body was against air. The cloth still covered my eyes, and my ears burned.

Horse was a good cow.

I said, Where am I.

There was another kick. A sole against my feet—pushing down, and my ear was squished against the wood. There was a slap. There was a fist. A sole against my ribs. There was a spit.

Stay strong, Horse.

I said, String cheese.

Stay shut, the voice said.

It was The Dirty Man's voice.

I said, Where's my Rain Crunch Chocolate and Vanilla Cookie.

I ate it all up, The Dirty Man said.

I said, It's good with a glass of milk.

It is, The Dirty Man said.

The sole kept pushing down on my face. My neck was ready to go. I was ready to go. He dragged me around the room, making all kinds of clinking and rattling sounds, as he yanked me into walls or cabinets or tables.

There was dripping.

There was a slap.

He pulled my ear. He pulled my nose. He flicked my forehead with his fingers.

No cookie for you here, The Dirty Man said.

I said, Kill me or let me go.

Too easy, The Dirty Man said.

There was wet against my face. He spat again. He spat again and again, and then he dragged me around the room. He liked to slap me.

I said, You're a lot stronger when I'm tied up and blindfolded.

You're going to witness pain like you've never seen, The Dirty Man said.

The door squeaked, and there were more footsteps. More kicks.

Look at this helpless bitch, the voice said. Always getting in the way, the voice said.

I said, Have we met.

I wasn't sure how much longer my ribs could last. I was having trouble breathing, too. I wasn't sure if it was sweat or blood or spit on my skin. Barn learned how to swim in ditches and levees. He had never been to a swimming pool. I always wanted to take him to one. Maybe Ma or Pepper would be able, or if I could make it, I would take him. He would love the diving board. I pictured him jumping off the diving board and never coming down.

I said, Floating in air.

The world felt vertical. My soles were to the floor. I was sitting upright again.

I said, How many of you all does it take to beat me up.

The world was horizontal again.

They were whispering to each other, and the whispering became louder, until there was a sssshhhh, and they lowered their voices again.

There was a hand against my face, pushing my face in, and the inside of my mouth was pressed against the gums and teeth. The fingers dug in deep, and the hand shook my head from side to side.

You're so cute, said the voice.

I tried to say something.

The voice made me vertical again. There was a hit on the back of my head.

You will see pain, The Dirty Man said.

You will hear pain, the voice said.

There will be a good fucking, The Dirty Man said.

I said, Sounds like a plan.

Horse. She was always so soothing. Barn could fall asleep to her moos. I could, too. She still had three good legs. The fourth leg didn't look too bad off, but she was hurting. I wondered how Barn would handle it when Horse passed away. We would give her a good burial. Barn would have a good chance to give her one last hug. It was just that there wouldn't be any more Horse licks to Barn's face anymore.

I said, Kill me or let me go.

They said something, but I wasn't really listening. I was thinking about Ma. I didn't think I was really all that helpful to her, but I did think she enjoyed my company. She was the only person I knew who loved me, who nurtured me, who taught me right. She didn't need me to keep going, but there was love.

Pepper didn't need me, either. I always wondered when she would just cut me off and not talk to me anymore. I didn't think it would last as long as it had, so far. I thought about her blue painted fingernails and her green painted toenails. When she smiled, it was a real good smile. When she was mad or angry or lost or drunk, it was a real good mad or angry or lost or drunk. She always went all out. She was never halfway. I was hoping that her stubbornness and tenacity would get her far, would get her away. One day, Ma and Barn and Pepper would be gone, taking care of the world, and I would be left here sleeping on Horse's grave.

They all would take me with them.

If I could make it out of here.

Let's go, the voice said.

I said, Where.

Pain, the voice said.

I said, That's west of here.

I was horizontal again. I was dragged again. From floor to floor to floor to concrete to grass to concrete. The door shut. I was horizontal. There was an engine. We were moving. The world was all dark. I tried to wrestle my arms free from the rope, and I tried to wrestle my legs free from the rope, but nothing worked.

You keep trying, The Dirty Man said.

I said, I'm hungry.

There were turns and stops, and I was sliding around. I remembered seeing a van at the gas station.

I said, Is the mumbling man here.

That'll be me, the voice said.

I said, Who was the third guy.

Just a pond in our plan, The Dirty Man said.

I said, Pond.

Dummy, The Dirty Man said. The Dirty Man said, Yeah. The Dirty Man said, Pond.

Chess, the voice said.

Pepper was good at checkers. I had never beaten her just like I had never beaten her in bowling. Maybe one day we could learn to play chess. Ma said she used to play a lot. Maybe Ma could teach us.

I said, Y'all play chess.

Nope, The Dirty Man said.

Nope, the voice said.

I said, Pond.

There was light. There was Pepper. Ache, ache, ache went the head. Pepper was tied up. She was facing me. I kept looking at her legs—tan and smooth and tempting. She wore a pink tank top. Her hair was a mess, partially covering her face. I could see her lips—they were bright red. There was her belly button. I wanted to lick it.

I said, Hi Pepper.

What the fuck is this, Pepper said.

I said, Your legs look great.

I just got out of the tub, Pepper said.

The Dirty Man said, Shut the fuck up.

There was The Dirty Man, and there was the employee from the gas station. He was still wearing his gray work shirt and black pants. He looked different. He had this sleazy tone to him. Before, I felt bad for him—he had this vulnerable look to him. But at Pepper's place, he looked like no good.

I said, String cheese.

No more string cheese, the employee said.

I looked at Pepper's breasts. Her nipples were poking.

I said, I got you string cheese.

Thanks, Pepper said.

The Dirty Man said, Shut the fuck up.

He slapped the back of my head, and kicked me in the shins.

Quit hitting me, I said.

Pepper laughed.

Pepper said, I'm the only one who's allowed to hit him.

She spat on The Dirty Man.

You're real pretty, the employee said.

The Dirty Man slapped Pepper. Pepper laughed.

You're real ugly, Pepper said. Pepper said, You look like a sick and pale dying frog.

The employee fixed his hair a bit and looked at his skin.

There was light. There was a love bug hovering between me and Pepper. I hadn't seen one in a while. Pepper was looking at it, too. The love bug landed on her knee.

It tickles, Pepper said.

The Dirty Man slapped her knee, and the love bug was squished against her skin.

There'll be plenty more, Pepper said.

The Dirty Man slapped her.

I said, Stop slapping everyone.

It's the only way they can take us, Pepper said. Pepper said, We have to be tied up because he isn't too strong.

I said, If Ma was here.

If Ma was here, Pepper said. Pepper said, These guys would already be knocked out.

We both laughed.

Bug, bug, bug went the love, and love, love, love went the bug. One, one, one went the two. Two, two, two went the one. None, none, none went the love, and one, one, one went the none.

How's your Pops, The Dirty Man said.

Pepper stopped laughing.

Pepper said, You tell me.

Oh he's good, The Dirty Man said. The Dirty Man said, He's doing real good. The Dirty Man said, He told me to tell you hi. The Dirty Man said, He told me to give you a peck on the cheek for him.

The Dirty Man walked up to Pepper and put his face right up to Pepper's. He breathed hard on her. Pepper didn't budge. She didn't flinch. The Dirty Man kissed her cheek.

That's from your Pops, The Dirty Man said.

He whispered something to her.

Pepper said, Come close. Pepper said, Give this to him. Pepper said, Tell him it's from me.

The Dirty Man licked his lips. He put his face back up to Pepper's. Pepper cleared her throat and spat in The Dirty Man's eyes.

I said, Here we go.

The Dirty Man pushed her over. I tired to make a move at him but I also fell over. The world was horizontal again. The employee put his foot on the side of my head.

Stay put, the employee said.

Pepper was sideways, too. She was looking right at me as The Dirty Man was kicking her. She wasn't shouting or screaming or crying. She was smiling.

I'm glad you're here with me, Pepper said. Pepper said, I'm usually alone.

I said, We'll get some string cheese.

The Dirty Man kicked her in the stomach. Pepper laughed.

Pepper said, You're a big and strong man.

The Dirty Man said, Come help.

The employee walked up to Pepper and The Dirty Man. No one loved pain more than Pepper. I was glad I was there to give her some comfort or company. She was having a good time. When The Dirty Man and the employee stopped, Pepper was covered in blood. I couldn't see her eyes, or her nose, or her lips. Her hair was red and tangled. Her pink shirt was red. Pepper was red. She didn't say anything. She wasn't moving.

You're next, The Dirty Man said.

I was next.

Pepper, Pepper, Pepper went the side. Red, red, red went the shirt. Blood, blood, blood went the face. More, more, more went the ribs. Head, head, head went the boots, Cheese, cheese, cheese, went the string.

There was something beautiful in the middle of all of this, and it was Pepper. Her hair had moved to the side, and I could see her eyes. She was looking right back at me. She looked like she wanted to cry. I smiled back and tried to say something.

Dark, dark, dark went the light, and light, light, light went the dark. Room, room, room went the thud. Spat, spat, spat went the spit. Dig, dig, dig went the soles. Breath, breath, breath went the mouth. Tongue, tongue, tongue went the gums.

Balloons and cotton candy, and the circus was in the sky, and there were love bugs and Horse, and the barn was open and full of clucking.

Cluck, cluck, cluck went Horse. Horse, Horse, Horse went the moo. Chair, chair, chair went the broke.

There was a slight bit of freedom mixed with red grunts and steel and soles. There were Pepper's eyes. She never looked away.

Stop, stop, stop went the sound. Loose, loose, loose went the ropes. Head, head, head went the whirl. Ring, ring, ring went the brain.

There was silence and hard breathing. The Dirty Man and the employee looked like they were tiring.

I said, Just think if we were untied.

You still alive, Pepper said.

I said, You look pretty sideways.

You look like a fool, Pepper said.

I said, Am I bloodier than you.

You look great, Pepper said.

We were both babbling, but we understood each other.

Am I bloodier than you, Pepper said.

I said, I think I'm winning.

I wonder what Barn is up to, Pepper said.

I said, Flying.

The hard breathing stopped. I could only see their legs. They paced around and back and forth in front of my eyes. The stitching on The Dirty Man's jeans was coming undone.

We are only just starting, The Dirty Man said.

I said, You need new jeans.

The Dirty Man stopped walking. The jean legs were pulled up a bit, and I could see his socks—they were black and red.

I've been meaning to get a new pair, The Dirty Man said.

I said, And new socks.

The employee lifted Pepper and made her vertical. I was vertical, too.

Rush, rush, rush went the arteries.

A little love, The Dirty Man said.

He lifted Pepper's chin.

A little love, The Dirty Man said.

Pepper said, Not even when I'm dead.

I said, Ghosts.

Pepper kept her mouth closed. Pepper kept her legs closed.

Just a little love, The Dirty Man said.

Pepper kept silent. The back of my chair was broken and one of the legs was wobbly. The rope had loosened, but I didn't want to get free while both the employee and The Dirty Man were still attentive.

Don't worry, The Dirty Man said. The Dirty Man said, Your Pops says it's okay. The Dirty Man said, He knows.

Pepper looked the other way.

I've been helping your dad, The Dirty Man said. You know that right, The Dirty Man said. This is just a little compensation, The Dirty Man said.

The employee was walking in circles.

Let's get going, the employee said. We got to go, the employee said.

He talks about you, The Dirty Man said.

Pepper looked at The Dirty Man. Her eyes were a bit watery. There was something there in her eyes.

He tells me how he used to hold you when you were a baby, The Dirty Man said. The Dirty Man said, He tells me how he taught you how to pack his smokes and how to shoot.

The Dirty Man ran his fingers across Pepper's thighs.

The Dirty Man ran his fingers through her hair.

You're all grown up now, The Dirty Man said. The Dirty Man said, Your Pops would be real proud of you. The Dirty Man said, The way you handle yourself.

He pinched Pepper's neck.

The Dirty Man said, Strong and stubborn. The Dirty Man said, Just like your little Mommy.

Pepper looked at me. She was trying hard not to give in. There were watery eyes, but there were no tears.

Where's your mamma, The Dirty Man said. Where's your mamma, The Dirty Man said.

He twirled with her hair. He played with her hair.

Your mamma isn't round anymore, The Dirty Man said. The Dirty Man said, What happened to your mamma.

Pepper's eyes were red. The water was no longer there. I kept looking at her. The employee was pacing in circles.

We got to go, the employee said.

The Dirty Man said, Shut it. The Dirty Man said, Not until I'm through here.

The employee crossed his arms and paced back and forth. He looked at his watch and then at The Dirty Man, and then at Pepper. He looked at me. I tried to shrug my shoulders but I was too tied up to make any kind of gesture.

I said, Sorry.

I'll tell you what happened to your mamma, The Dirty Man said. The Dirty Man said, I'll tell you right now. The Dirty Man said, And your sweet little friend here will know, too.

He lifted Pepper's chin.

He pinched her cheeks, making her lips stick out. He put his lips up close, but Pepper shook her head and The Dirty Man lost his grip. She bit his chin. The Dirty Man screamed.

Pepper laughed.

Your Pops says I should be gentle with you, The Dirty Man said. Your Pops says you'll come around if I just wait. The Dirty Man said, Well I'm not waiting around anymore. The Dirty Man said, Once I'm through with you and your friend here, I'll be through with your Pops, too.

The Dirty Man unbuckled his belt and whipped Pepper on the legs. He whipped her arms, too. He whipped her body and her hands and feet. I looked at her toes. They were scraping the floor. She was trying her best not to scream, but she just couldn't take it anymore. I screamed with her.

The employee took off. He ran straight out the door without shutting it.

Fuckin' coward, The Dirty Man said. The Dirty Man said, He's got a lot of growing up to do. The Dirty Man said, He's got a lot to learn.

He moved his hips in circles like he was doing aerobics.

Pepper looked at me. Whether she was thinking about doing it or not, I didn't wait to find out. I slid my arms over the broken back of the chair. My hands were still tied, and my legs were still tied so I had to hop over to The Dirty Man.

I put my arms over his head and pushed his head back and started to choke him. Pepper used her head to hit him in the stomach. I had a strong enough grip around his neck to push him hard against the wall. As soon as he hit the wall, I ran right into him with my shoulder, over and over again. And when he was on the ground, I kept jumping on top of him until he stopped moving. With more time now, I was able to go the kitchen and get a knife and cut the rope free from my legs and arms.

Free.

I said, Gun.

Tampons, Pepper said.

I went to the bathroom and found the pistol in the cabinet drawer. Pepper was free, too. The Dirty Man started to move around. Pepper went after him. She kicked him and scratched him, and punched him. She was really giving it to him—possessed and not of this earth. After a few minutes, I pulled her away.

I said, Take a break.

The Dirty Man wasn't moving. The door slammed open and the employee ran in. I gave Pepper the gun, and she pointed it at him. The employee tried to run back out but a goat came in through the door, blocking his way, and caused him to trip over the coffee table.

I said, There's that goat.

Good goat, Pepper said.

The employee got back up and started shooting as us. There were shots. Me and Pepper took cover in the kitchen, behind the counter. Pepper shot back. The goat was frolicking around the living room.

I said, Everyone has a gun except me.

It he hits that goat, Pepper said.

There was silence. The goat bleated. The employee was dragging The Dirty Man across the floor and towards the door. There were more shots. The employee and The Dirty Man were gone. The goat was alive in the living room, nudging its head against the sofa.

Pepper got a few beers from the fridge for me, and the goat, and herself. We sat there and drank one after another. The pain was still there, but the head felt good. The goat was wobbling around and then rested on the floor, licking its arms and legs. We stared at the goat until our eyes closed, and when we woke up, the goat was gone. Pepper still had the gun in one hand and a beer in the other, with her head resting against the wall.

I nudged her and her head fell down. She popped it back up and her eyes were open.

I said, Head hurts.

Head hurts, Pepper said.

I said, We should go. I said, Before they get back. I said, We need some rest.

I'm ready, Pepper said.

I said, I bet Ma has got something good in the kitchen.

I'm hungry, Pepper said.

We got up and kicked some of the broken things out the way.

I said, This place is broken.

It was always broken, Pepper said.

I said, Let's let Ma take care of us.

Your Ma is good, Pepper said.

We put our arms around each other's shoulders and walked out the door. It was bright, bright, bright.

BREAD PUDDING

Ma was fixing us up. She was quiet and worked fast. Her hands were soft and gentle. Her eyes were fixed on our cuts and bruises and aches, making sure she covered every bit of hurt skin. She took care of Pepper, and then she took care of me. Barn watched the whole time, either tugging of Ma's muumuu or my shirt, or Pepper's shorts. Barn had this face I hadn't seen before.

It'll be okay, we all said.

I looked at the bathroom mirror and saw Pepper. I was her. I wondered if she was me. I looked at the bathroom mirror and saw myself. I wondered if I was me. Pepper came in from behind and looked at the mirror. She touched my face and my shoulders and ribs and grimaced with each touch.

Ma said that Pepper wasn't going back home anymore. She said that Pepper was going to stay with us until everything was cleaned and clear. Pepper didn't argue.

I said, It's like a family.

I don't know what that is, Pepper said.

I said, It's you, and Barn, and Ma, and me.

Sounds fun, Pepper said.

She brushed my hair back.

I said, Are you me.

I am, Pepper said.

I said, We are each other.

We, Pepper said.

Ma went to the store and got some clothes for Pepper. She didn't tell Pepper about it. She also got her some make-up and a toothbrush. When she got back from the store and showed Pepper what she got her, Pepper gave Ma a big hug and started trying on the clothes in the living room. Ma also got Barn a rocket, and she said she was going to make bread pudding for dessert—my favorite.

I said, I owe you a slushie.

Where's my slushie, Ma said.

I said, I'll get one for you.

And those mint cookies, Ma said.

Ma stayed strong when she was taking care of us. She didn't show any worry. She didn't lecture us about being careful. She knew we knew. She didn't say that she was going to the cops. She knew that wasn't going to do anything. She didn't make us stay at home but let us go out into the field or to the store or a restaurant. She didn't show it on her face, but one night when everyone was sleeping, I went to the fridge to get some late night bread pudding, and I saw Ma sitting out in the back, and she was crying.

OUT ON THE FIELD

Pepper was sitting on the hood of the tractor. She had her clothes on. We were well into the night, and we put on the headlights to lose ourselves in the wavering motions of the gnats hovering around the bright bulbs.

They'll be back, Pepper said.

She was playing with her hair, twirling it around in circles. Before the sun went down, I was studying her face as she was daydreaming. I was looking at every scratch, every bruise, every scab.

I said, We'll get them.

Mamma, Pepper said.

I look out into the darkness of the field, where nothing could be seen. There was distant barking. It was a black ocean, the field at night, and it was easy to get lost in it—to drown in it and never come back.

I said, She was good.

She was good, Pepper said.

I didn't want to ask her much about her mom, not because I didn't care or didn't want to know, but it was something that Pepper would talk about only if she wanted to talk about it.

I said, Your dad.

He was good at one time, Pepper said.

I said, Kind of like Uncle Gerald.

Mamma and Dad were apple pie, Pepper said.

I said, Your mom is still alive.

And then it got all rotten, Pepper said.

She stopped talking after that. We just sat there and watched the flying bugs dance in the light and listened to the dogs barking. I put my hand on her shoulder and she didn't push it away. We were all sore.

Ma was in the living room with Barn. Uncle Gerald had sent a letter to his son, and Ma was reading the letter out loud to Barn.

Ma said, Sit Barn.

Barn sat.

Ma was in the recliner, rocking it back and forth. Barn was on the couch, fidgeting and shuffling around. He never really liked to sit in one spot. I sat down next to him and listened to Ma.

Ma said, Dear Barn. Ma said, I have done plenty of wrong things in my life. Ma said, I've made plenty of mistakes. Ma said, But the worst mistake I made. Ma said, The only real regret I have. Ma said, Is leaving you.

This is from your dad, I said.

Barn stopped moving around. Like a dog, it looked like his ears lifted.

Ma said, Lil' Barn. Ma said, You're something beautiful. Ma said, You are a little ball of energy and wonder. Ma said, And I wish I was around to see you grow. Ma said, I wouldn't be too much of a father. Ma said, I don't think I would be good at teaching you how to grow up. Ma said, But instead, I would learn from you.

Barn started to look around the living room. Ma was having a bit of a rough time reading the letter. She was always pausing and thinking. It really got to her.

He's not here Barn, I said. It's a letter, I said. He wrote a letter to you, I said.

Barn kept looking at the window.

Ma said, Take care of your aunt, my sister. Ma said, Take care of your Mutty. Ma said, And always do good. Ma said, Don't be like your dad. Ma said, I will write to you again soon. Ma said, As much as you should forget about me. Ma said, Here is a photo of us.

Ma held up a photo to the light coming from the window. She sighed.

Ma said, Look Barn.

Barn took the photo. He twisted it around. He held it upside down. He held it right-side up. He held it face down. And then he looked at the photo. He ran his fingers across the glossy surface. I looked at it, too. It was a photo of Uncle Gerald and Barn on the banks of a river. Barn was holding a catfish. Uncle Gerald was wearing jeans and a camouflage jacket. His eyes were gentle, full of joy—much unlike the photo in the newspaper after he had escaped prison.

I said, Did you catch that. I said, Did you catch that catfish.

Barn started moving again. He ran around the living room, hopping and skipping.

He was good at fishing, Ma said.

DRIVING AROUND WITH PEPPER

Me and Pepper were driving around in the truck. Pepper was at the wheel. She was barefoot and whistling.

I said, Can you sing.

Like a frog, Pepper said.

I said, Sing.

Fuck you, Pepper said.

I said, Keep whistling.

Pepper stopped whistling. We were on our way to the gardening center to pick up some flowers and plants for Ma, but Pepper took a right somewhere.

I said, Shortcut.

You'll see, Pepper said.

We were in town. Pepper kept driving, stopping and going, stopping and going. The were so many traffic lights—things that weren't usually seen in the countryside. In the country, the cows and goats were the traffic lights.

The part of the town we were in was run down. A lot of broken stores and signs and roads. A lot of broken people. A lot of broken cars and lights and windows.

I said, Pretty.

Pepper kept driving until she got to an intersection. There was a four-way stop sign.

Five Corners, Pepper said.

I looked around and only saw four corners.

Mamma used to sing, Pepper said.

She turned on the window wipers though it was completely dry outside. They squeaked against the window.

Pollen, Pepper said.

There were still some remnants of dirt in the truck from when we went muddin'. I threw some chunks out the window. Pepper pointed to a broken down bar. The neon light sign on the window was broken. Someone was walking into it. At the top there was a sign that read, Jazz And Blus and Booz. The 'e' was missing from the last two words.

I said, Every Friday night.

Mamma used to sing to me, Pepper said. She had a voice that could have been on the radio, Pepper said. But she never really tried to make it big, Pepper said.

The car behind us honked. Pepper stuck her hand out and motioned for the car to pass us up.

Mamma would sing me to sleep, Pepper said. Mamma would sing to me to wake me up, Pepper said. Mamma would always be singing.

I said, Where'd she go.

She's gone, Pepper said.

I said, Mississippi.

Pepper shook her head. She started to drive again and turned around to go back to the gardening center.

Her and Dad were good together, Pepper said.

She sank low into the driver's seat with her head back against the headrest.

There was laughing, Pepper said. And there were smiles, Pepper said.

I said, Rotten.

And then Dad got into some bad things, Pepper said. And Mamma went along with him, Pepper said.

I said, She's in prison.

Pepper shook her head. She stopped talking about them after that.

At the gardening center, we bought pots of gerbera daisies and sunflowers and marigolds. Pepper ate some of the petals.

I said, Save some of them for the garden.

They're just too good, Pepper said.

She handed me a petal.

Paint your tongue, Pepper said.

I put it in my mouth and sucked on it.

When we got home and showed Ma the flowers, she got excited and started to plant them in front of the house.

The house needed some new energy, Ma said.

I said, Colors.

Barn tried to help, too, but he kept getting distracted with the ladybugs. Like Pepper, he ended up eating some of the petals, too.

It'll spoil your appetite, Ma said.

She held out her hand in front of Barn's mouth, and Barn spat out some of the chewed up petals.

Pepper said, Tastes good.

When we were done, the garden in the front yard brightened up the house. Pepper and Ma were watering it and they were talking to each other. I didn't hear what they were talking about

111

and I didn't really want to hear what they were talking about. It was good so see that they were having some time together without me. Ma would move her head up and down and gesture with her hands, and Pepper would do the same. Everything looked bright.

Pepper had snuck off. She didn't tell Ma or me where she was going. Maybe she told Barn, but Barn would never tell us. I drove around looking for her. I went into town first, and went to the bowling alley, the arcade, the movie theater, and the gardening center. I kept a lookout for her red truck but I didn't see anything.

I thought about The Dirty Man, the mumbling man, and the employee. I drove past the gas station and wondered if he still worked there. It must have been just a one night thing. He probably never worked there. There was a police car at the gas station, too, and me and Ma had talked about going to the police but we both knew nothing would get done.

They're more crooked than my teeth, Ma said.

I said, Dentures.

Most probably, The Dirty Man or the mumbling man or the employee had an in with some of the cops because if they didn't, they shouldn't really be free right now.

I drove to Pepper's place, out in the fields, and went inside her house. Her truck wasn't there, but I went in anyway. The place was still trashed, but the wandering goat was there, keeping guard. I gave it a beer and had one for myself, too. There was a trail of ants on the kitchen counter, near the microwave—they were marching towards some crumbs. I followed the trail and climbed through the kitchen window, and there was an ant pile that almost came up to my knees. Pepper would have stuck her feet right in if she was there. I didn't touch the ants on the counter but I cleaned up the kitchen and threw away anything that was accessible or edible. I gave some of it to the goat, too. Eventually, the ants would get bored and find another place to haunt, I thought.

As I was walking back to the truck, I pictured Pepper singing and then the Jazz And Blus And Booz sign entered my mind.

I said, Good thought.

Pepper was there, sitting at the bar, staring at the racks of liquor bottles in front of her. It was just her and the bartender. The place was dark, and it seemed darker after walking in from the daylight, and I ran into a table as my eyes adjusted. Neither Pepper nor the bartender turned their heads.

There were a few tables and some chairs facing a slightly elevated stage. There was just a microphone stand on the stage and on the sides of the space, there were some bundled up curtains. As dirty as the place looked—with empty beer bottles and glasses everywhere, along with ashtrays full of butts, and there were some on the floor, too—it didn't smell too bad. It smelled like home.

I went up to the bar and sat next to Pepper, asking for a beer from the bartender. Pepper still didn't look at me. She knew I was going to find her. I almost tapped her on the shoulder but I kept my hands on the counter. The bartender gave me a bottle and lit Pepper's cigarette. She blew the smoke up, towards the ceiling without taking her eyes off the rack of liquor bottles in front of her.

I said, Pepper.

Mutty, Pepper said.

She was sipping out of a straw—her glass was empty.

I said, Hammer.

Screwdriver, Pepper said.

The bartender fixed her another drink. I breathed in the smoke that she was blowing out and kept it in my lungs for a few seconds before letting it go.

I said, There's an ant pile next to your kitchen that comes up to your knees.

Did you stick your feet in it, Pepper said.

I said, The goat is still there.

That's a good goat, Pepper said.

She turned and looked at me. Even in the dark room, I could see her red eyes. Her head was wobbly. Her hands weren't there. Her body had no bones. She pointed at a bottle on the rack.

Mamma, Pepper said.

It was a bottle of gin.

That was her drink, Pepper said.

She told me that her mom would sometimes take her to the bar when she didn't want to leave Pepper home alone, and how she would sit at the side of the stage and watch her mom sing, and then when it was all over, they would stay after-hours, and Pepper would watch her mom talk and drink and laugh. Pepper pointed at a lounge chair near the stage.

Sometimes I would fall asleep there, Pepper said.

Sometimes, Pepper went on to say, her dad would be there too, and Pepper remembered seeing him mouth the words that her mom was singing. Sometimes, he would take Pepper's hands and they would dance around the room.

114

All I could see were knees, Pepper said.

Pepper lit another cigarette even though the one she was smoking was still lit. She got up and started wavering around the room. She looked like ballet. The bartender put on some music, and the place sounded more alive.

I got up and grabbed Pepper's hands and danced around with her. We were running into chairs and tables and knocking over empty glasses and bottles, but not because Pepper was drunk and uncontrollable, but because I didn't know how to dance. I could feel the beer sloshing around in my stomach.

Follow me, Pepper said.

I looked at her eyes. They were closed. She knew where she was though. I kept my eyes opened but followed her movements, her hands, as they guided me around her and around the room.

Legs, legs, legs went the heels. Hands, hands, hands went the twirl. La, la, la went Pepper. Beer, beer, beer went the slosh.

Everything was a whirl.

Pepper's cigarette never left the tip of her lips. It looked like it was ready to fall, but it just bounced in perfect motion with Pepper's body.

I said, Ballet.

Waltz, Pepper said.

I said, Matilda.

We went on the stage and danced around the microphone stand. Pepper untied the curtains, and they fluttered open, and we tangled ourselves in the velvet cloth. Pepper never lost her step, and I bumped her a few times, but she didn't say anything. She was in her own world. I was guessing that this world existed years ago when Pepper had a good memory.

The song faded away, and before the next song started, Pepper opened her red eyes and looked around. They were glossy—a thin sheet of water covered them, and I wanted to splash.

The bartender clapped and cheered.

Encore, the bartender said.

Pepper bowed and blew kisses.

Take a bow, Pepper said.

I bowed.

Blow kisses, Pepper said.

I blew kisses.

Pepper clapped and cheered.

You all have been so lovely, Pepper said. Pepper said, The

world rotates in rhythms and let us never forget these songs.

I clapped.

In these songs, Pepper said. Pepper said, There is sadness and happiness. Pepper said, And they keep the world singing and dancing.

Pepper bowed again. I bowed again.

Pepper said, One more drink.

Hammer, I said.

Pepper said, And then I want to take you somewhere.

I said, You've taken me everywhere.

Pepper said, There is one hidden hole you haven't seen.

We sat back down at the bar. The bartender seemed to have to have taken a liking to me after the dance with Pepper, and the drinks were on him.

Pepper lit another cigarette and looked at the gin bottle.

I said, You're grinning.

It won't be for long, Pepper said.

MAMMA'S GRAVE

We were in the parking lot, walking towards the truck.
I'm driving, Pepper said.
I said, I'll drive.
I'm not drunk, Pepper said.
I said, I am.
She gave me the keys. She gave me directions. We were back in the country—where both of us felt most at home, most comfortable. The sun was midway, and the sky was a slushie.
Keep going, I said.
Pepper said, Until you see a lantern.
Light, I said.
We drove for about thirty minutes. I had never been to this side of the town before. We all lived in fields and hay, but this side of town had no sign of lights and electricity and people. There weren't really any cows in the field, either. Every now and then, there was a pasture, but the grass was empty. Pepper was quiet. Her head was still wobbly and her eyes were still red. She hummed and snapped her fingers every now and then. And when she wasn't doing that, she stuck her hand out the window and let the air slap her palm. She stuck her head out at times, too—with her tongue out and her eyes closed.
Lantern, I said.
Pepper said, Right there.
I took a right into the gravel driveway.
Pepper said, Don't pull up all the way.
The house had columns in the front. The yard was wide and long, and there weren't any houses next to it. There was a lantern just on the edge of the road, near the mailbox. There weren't any lights on in the house. There weren't any lights on anywhere— there were only the crickets and the croaks.
I don't think they're home, I said.
Pepper said, Home.
Is something we don't know, I said.
Pepper said, Give me the keys.
Pepper played around with the keys until she found the one she was looking for. The door opened. It was hot and thick inside. I coughed. Pepper turned on the light.
Pepper said, Everything.

117

There were frames on the wall. There was a young Pepper. There was a family. There was a pretty woman, a handsome man. There was a vase on the table in the living room. There was furniture. There was a previous life here.

Pepper walked into the kitchen. The fridge was off. The cabinets and the pantry were empty. Just behind the sink was a handprint made out of uncooked macaroni. Pepper put her hand up to it. She walked out and went into another room.

There was nothing there. No bed or dresser or anything. None of the rooms had anything. There was only the living room and the hallway walls that had signs of memories. Pepper lay on the carpet and rubbed her hands against the floor. There was a spider on the wall.

Hermit, I said.

I coughed.

Come, Pepper said. Pepper said, Let's get some fresh air.

I followed her to a back door. The patio light highlighted the beginnings of an endless field.

Pepper said, It's like sleeping.

She took my hand and we walked a good bit on the field. At some points, she started to jog, and then at other times, she slowed down.

Pepper said, Here.

There was a mound. There was stone. It all looked like one big clump, and after staring at it for a while, it started to float, making it all look like a ghost.

Pepper kneeled down and patted the mound. She brushed away some weeds and dirt, and patted it again. She took my hand and motioned me to do the same. The soil was cold and fresh. Pepper put her nose to it and smelled it. She rubbed her hand against the stone and kissed it.

Hi Mamma, Pepper said.

I said, Hi there.

One night, Pepper said. Pepper said, Dad walked into the house. Pepper said, He had been gone for days. Pepper said, Mamma left one day just saying, I'm going to get your Dad.

She was on her back now, looking up at the glittery sky. I was doing the same. I could hear the tall grass ruffling as she moved her legs around.

One night, Pepper said. Pepper said, Dad walked into the house and told me that Mamma wasn't coming back. Pepper said,

He was holding her, bloody and limp. Pepper said, Her hair was fixed nice and she looked pretty.

She stopped moving her legs and arms and remained quiet for a while. I didn't say anything either and just listened to the bugs.

Pepper said, I helped Dad bury her here. Pepper said, Dad never told me what happened. Pepper said, Dad told me that if I knew that, I could be buried right next to Mamma.

Pepper thought that she got caught up in her dad's gang, and something didn't match, and she ended up getting it. She also thought that maybe her mom was in the same situation that she was in with The Dirty Man, and that her mom ended up dead, and that maybe she would end dead.

I'm sure I'm supposed to be dead, Pepper said.

I said, Let's get some food.

Barn was walking on his hands. He could do it for about six seconds before toppling over. I could do it for just about the same amount of time. Pepper could go much longer—about eleven seconds. She was trying to teach Barn about balance and how to maintain body control. We were out in the backyard.

Ma was inside. Through the window, I could see her in her recliner, smoking a cigarette and drinking something out of a cup.

I said, Barn.

Barn looked at me upside down. I tilted my head.

I said, Go get Ma.

Barn ran inside and came back out holding Ma's hand. Ma had the cigarette in her mouth, still holding the cup.

I said, Handstands.

Ma shrugged her shoulders.

I'll put all of you to shame, Ma said. Ma said, Including you Pepper.

Barn clapped his hands. She put the cup on the ground, but kept the cigarette in her mouth and got on her hands—kicking her legs up. She did it too hard and flipped over. Barn jumped up and down.

Fuck, Ma said.

Pepper said, We all have been shamed.

Another go, Ma said.

She flipped over again.

Barn and I went again and lasted for a good bit. Pepper walked halfway through the backyard on her hands. As we were all in the backyard, watching each other doing handstands and cursing, I looked up at the sun and saw a spot somewhere between the yard and the sky. It was a black spot, moving slowly. I looked at Pepper, and Ma, and Barn. I looked at the black spot.

I said, One day.

For those few minutes, in our own little world, we were the black spot. But we always had to come back. We were grounded. I was just waiting for that point when we didn't have to come back down, when we were the black spot and never-ending.

Up and up and up. Side and side and side. Down and down and down. Upside and upside and upside. Downside and downside and downside. Gravity and gravity and gravity. Grave, grave, grave. Spot and spot and spot. Soar and soar and soar. Palm, palm, palm.

This was the way the world went in the backyard.

GOOD AND BAD

There were bad things. Bad people. Leave us alone. There was good and smiles and laughing but it always had to be erased. Leave us alone.

Pepper acted like it was just normal. Standard. She was bothered by it just as much as she was bothered by traffic or a flat tire. Pepper actually liked flat tires. She could change them pretty fast, much faster than me. Whenever she would hold the spare, her tight biceps, covered in sweat, pierced everything around her.

There were bad things. Bad people. They knew no other way. They grew up to be bad. Bad Ma. Bad Dad. Dads, cousins and uncles and relatives. If they saw good, would they be bad or good? Bad made them feel good. Good made them feel scared.

Pepper would be scared, too—when she was happy and having a good time. She wasn't used to it. One time I asked her if she had any friends, and she looked at me like I had asked her the dumbest question. But then she answered.

I've only had three friends, Pepper said.

I said, Besides us.

Only y'all, Pepper said.

I said, How does it feel.

I don't like it, Pepper said.

I said, We can go.

No, Pepper said. Pepper said, I don't like it because I don't feel like I deserve it.

I said, You're no good.

No bad, no bad, no bad, Pepper said.

Every now and then I would catch her singing in the barn or to Barn. She never did it around anyone else—the closest would be humming or whistling. I still couldn't whistle. I would just spit and blow.

The farm was soothed with Pepper around. The animals, the grass, the house and the family—it was all gentle and comforted. Ma had always done a good job with the place and with us, and now with Pepper, it was like we were all in bed and falling asleep without tossing or turning. That was good for Ma. She was always tossing and turning. And the same went for Pepper. She would fall asleep as soon as she got into bed, or sometimes as soon as she lay down on the couch and closed her eyes, she was already dreaming.

Everyone was nails. We all kept each other together. Sometimes the nails would loosen or fall out, but we would always put them back in and hammer them tight. Barn was the best at this. Sometimes, I would see Pepper looking far off into the distance, wanting or waiting, I never knew, but then Barn would come up to her, and she would pick him up and get lost in Barn instead. We were all lost—Ma, Barn, Pepper, and me—but what made it good was that we were all lost together. What would it feel like if we were all found together?

What if Pierre was here? What if Pierre had never left? Would I feel more complete? Would I feel more like a man being around a man all the time? I didn't miss him or want him around. There was some good in Pierre. He just got confused. Ma had put in all the hard work, and she got all the credit. But what I wondered about the most was that if Pierre was around, maybe Ma would have been happier. Maybe she wouldn't rock back and forth in the recliner, chain smoking and falling asleep. I did my best to change things up for her. We did our best to change things up for her. And I knew she liked it and enjoyed it. But when it comes down to it, at the end of the day, when she went to bed—there was always a cold pillow next to her.

MAGIC

Walk, walk, walk, and walk, walk, walk, and walk, walk, walk. Sun, sun, sun went the field. Weeds, weeds, weeds went the knees. Tips, tips, tips went the fingers. Grass, grass, grass went the bronze. Toes, toes, toes went the soil. Sink, sink, sink went the heels.

Horse was there. Horse was good.

Moo, moo, chew went Horse. Horse, horse, horse went the hay. Leaf, leaf, leaf went the green. Oak, oak, oak went the shade. Chew, chew, moo went Horse. Horse, Horse, Horse went the hoof.

Pile, pile, pile went the ants.

There was a kingdom—full of dirt and antennae, and it was quiet and busy. The ants and their legs, their thoraxes and mandibles, could hold one crumb and the world.

Dream, dream, dream went the head and color, color, color went the earth. Sky, sky, sky went the spot, and spot, spot, spot went the gone.

In between the blades, there was a sparkle. The blades weren't sharp and shiny, but the sparkles were full of worms and clay and manure.

Chain, chain, chain went the clink. Tractor, tractor, tractor went the yellow. Push, push, push, went the earth.

Stung by a wasp in the dark—not a watt of sunlight to shine down on my neck, I cursed the night and rubbed my skin and yawned. I jumped up and down; I put my hands against the grass and pushed. I spat. I tied a rope around a branch of an oak and pulled back—it broke and I tumbled over. My eyes watered. I rolled around on the ground and chewed clovers, moaning and humming. I pulled my hair and stuck my tongue out.

Abracadabra. Abracadabra. Abracadabra.

For a minute.

For a minute, I needed everything to stop. I was no magician.

Poles, poles, poles went the go. Row, row, row went the axis. Stop, stop, stop went the try.

There was nothing. The travels of it all kept coming and going, and we had to go along with it.

TWO

Will you be going away.
When you don't see me, I'm away.
Will you be back after you leave.
I'll be back.
Come see us.
It will be the reason why I'll be back.
Why will you be going.
To make it better for all of us.
When will you be going away.
When no one is around.
There is a lot of sun.
It's bright.
You're bright.
I'll kill you.
Kill me.
You're trembling.
I am.
I've never seen you tremble before.
Usually it's you trembling.
Why are you trembling.
I'm not scared.
Why are you trembling like a wet dog.
I hear trumpets.
There are trumpets.
It is sad and lonely.
The trumpets speak from the lungs.
From something we can't hold.
You are trembling like a wet dog.
Sometimes I look at you and shake.
Let's dissect ourselves.
Let's break ourselves down.
There are veins.
There are arteries.
There are the organ keys.
Intestines.
Elbows.
Belly buttons and tongues.
Throats.

There are cells and bones.
Here are our fingers.
There is your nose.
Strings and threads.
And skin.
We have salt and we have oxygen.
You have eyes.
There are those lines on your palms.
Did you ever wonder what those are for.
It has something to do with the future.
Look at thighs.
Look at my opening.
Look at me.
There is the puzzle piece.
We fit.

I got Ma a slushie. She slurped it in two minutes. It was all gone.

Twinkle, Ma said.

There was a knock on the door.

I said, Pierre.

Damn it, Ma said.

Pierre said, Laurennette.

You got your damn chicken, Ma said.

Pierre said, Laurennette.

You got your chicken, I said.

Pierre said, Allow me to introduce myself.

We know who you are, I said.

Ma said, You're an idiot.

Pierre tried to walk in. Ma pushed him back out.

Talk, Ma said.

Pepper came into the living room holding Barn's hand.

Lil' Barn, Pierre said. Pierre said, Your dad misses you.

Barn looked around the room. Ma shut the door on Pierre. There was a knock.

I said, Pierre.

Laurennette, Pierre said.

Ma said, I'm not having it.

Where's the lady in the jean shorts, I said.

Pierre looked behind him. He shrugged his shoulders.

Pierre said, I think she's fishing.

Ma tried to shut the door again but Pierre stuck his hand out.

Let me sit, Pierre said.

He looked at Pepper and at Barn. He looked at me and Pepper. He took off his hat.

It's valid, Pierre said.

Ma moved inside. Pierre nodded his head and walked in. He sat in the recliner.

Ma said, Move.

Pierre got up and sat on the sofa.

Ma said, Shoes.

Pierre took them off. Ma sat in the recliner. Barn sat next to Pierre on the sofa. Me and Pepper stood.

Looks like, Pierre said. Pierre said, Y'all are going to be dead.

Ma said, Figures.

I'm hearing things, Pierre said.

Pepper said, I am, too.

I looked at her and put my hand on her shoulder.

Real voices, I said.

Pierre said, That's right. Pierre said, I'm hearing real voices.

Barn raised his eyebrows—his eyes were wide and round.

Don't you worry, Pepper said.

Pierre said, Brody.

The Dirty Man, I said.

Pierre shook his head. Pepper started swaying side to side with her arms crossed.

Ma said, No matter.

The ceiling fan started to squeak and shake. Barn looked up at it and started moving his head in motion with the wooden blades. Ma lit a cigarette. Pepper took one and lit it. Pierre took out his dip.

Ma said, Not in my house.

He put it back in his pocket. There was a rooster's crow. We all looked around.

Ma said, Insomnia.

There was a meow. There was a meow. There was a meow. There was a bark. There was a bark. There was a meow and a bark.

Brody has got it bad for y'all, Pierre said.

Ma said, We're going to have to take it to him this time.

No more waiting, Pepper said.

Barn nodded his head.

Pierre said, There's going to be more than blood.

He took out his can of dip and started packing it against his palm.

Pierre said, There's going to be bodies.

Either us or them, I said.

Pierre nodded his head.

Pierre said, Just a warning. Pierre said, This is a loose hurricane coming.

Ma said, We are a reckoning.

Pierre said, Get your gears. Pierre said, You might want to get the cops on this.

No good, Pepper said.

Pierre put some dip in his mouth. Ma got him a paper cup. I took some, too. The burning felt good. The gums felt good. I was buzzing already.

Ma said, Keep the gun on you at all times.

Under the pillow, Pierre said.

I said, They know where we live.

If they don't, Pierre said. Pierre said, They can find out.

Ma said, What do you have in all of this.

He's no good, Pierre said. Pierre said, Just wanted to protect.

Ma said, Why.

Family, Pierre said.

I said, Broken.

My fault, Pierre said.

Barn shuffled over and sat on Pierre's lap. Pierre took him in. Ma was about to say something but rubbed her arm instead. I liked how Barn had taken a good feeling towards him. It was a good sign. He had a good way of sensing what's good and what's bad. He was playful when things were good and he was wary and curious when things were bad.

Pierre spat.

They got a plan, Pierre said.

I said, Banks.

One big one, Pierre said.

Ma said, But why are they after us.

Pierre looked at Pepper. Ma looked at Pepper. I looked at Pepper. Barn was playing with the can of dip. He put it up to his nose and sniffed and made a sour face.

Ma said, We did nothing wrong.

Wrong doesn't matter, Pierre said. Pierre said, Sometimes bad looks over everything.

It's all my fault, Pepper said.

She sat down on the arm of the sofa and looked down.

I'm sorry, Pepper said.

I shook my head.

You did nothing wrong, Ma said.

I should get going, Pepper said. Pepper said, I should handle this. Pepper said, I should take care of this.

Ma said, We should take care of this.

I'm going to find them, Pepper said.

I said, We're going to find them.

No, Pepper said.

She looked at Barn. She stood up and looked at me and Ma.

Fuck off, Pepper said.

She patted Barn on the head.

Pierre stood up.

Why don't you just get, Pierre said. Pierre said, Leave this place.

He spat.

Can't be forced out of my own home, Pepper said. Pepper said, Won't have it.

I said, It's like pulling a turtle's body out from its shell and throwing it across the yard.

Something, Pepper said.

Pepper walked around for a bit and then left the living room. Pierre sat back down.

Ma said, Why'd you sit back down.

Just one more thing, Pierre said.

Ma shook her head and puffed.

Just one more chicken, Pierre said.

Ma sighed. She looked at me and nodded.

Ma said, You did good, Pierre.

I went off to get Pierre a chicken.

We licked cans and let the drips drop to our tongues. We closed our eyes and tilted our heads, looking up, letting the beams press down on our faces. The rooster's crow and the dog's meow beat against our skin. We were one. One was two. The green, and the green, and the green—it went on forever, and the leaves and the blades sharpened the air.

Sharp, sharp, sharp went the space. Soft, soft, soft went the manure. Day, day, day went the hours. Beam, beam, beam went the pores.

We swallowed and looked around and let the storm crash over our heads. Our arms stayed by our sides. In between the silence, there was thunder, and in between the thunder, there was us. We counted the seconds, and the sky split as we blinked.

Sky, sky, sky went the split. Rain, rain, rain went the heat. Dirt, dirt, dirt went the mud. Far, far, far went the howling.

We stayed together and let the water simmer. Mirages of lightning—it was there and then it was gone. We tried to grab it, but we only caught ourselves. We looked, and looked some more—looked, looked, looked—we looked until nothing could be seen, and it was here where angry spots of light could be found, wavering and colliding, making such a deafening sound, we held our breaths until the air stopped hurting.

We bit our tongues and each looked the other way and somewhere in the middle, there would be confusion. Looking at the stars, we played connect the dots and saw legs, arms, stomachs, lips, and eyes—the body of the universe.

Soar, soar, soar, our heads went—licking aluminum and pretending we were someone we recognized. She was me, and I was her. And when we looked at each other, our fingertips touched. This was something grand.

Grand, and grand, and grand.

There was gravel in our minds, and we shook our heads until the gray parted, and the mouths opened. Our mouths. And the mouths that couldn't be touched.

Grip, grip, grip went the hands. Hold, hold, hold went the hands. Tangle, tangle, tangle went the hands. Clasp, clasp, clasp went the hands. Hands, hands, hands went the hands.

We mumbled our mouths and talked about the emptiness. We

wondered what would happen next, after it was all finished. We had nothing. We had everything. We had puddles. And there was a wind, and the wind blew and our heads rocked back as we felt each other's skin. We felt ourselves.

It was a storm.

We stepped back.

Our clothes littered the fields, looking like kites, until they got so drenched, they sunk into the earth. We recycled our looks and slapped each other's thighs. Naked. We learned about being naked. And our skin blended with the drops, and the drips blended with our skin.

No, no, no went the yes. Yes, yes, yes, went the no. Shook, shook, shook went the nod, and scrunch, scrunch, scrunch went the shoulders.

Our shoulders and backs—tickled and full of bumps. Little bits and pieces our ourselves in each other's throats and our tongues tipped the tongues.

It helped us to feel.

Feel, feel, feel went the buds.

The roofs our mouths were coated. Bare and open, our bodies were turned towards the rain and the sun. Only here could there be such a mixture, during such a calm and frantic hour.

We were kettles clattering on the stove. Let the water boil over. Let the spout whistle. We didn't know the future and we barely knew the past. What was going on? The way the sky looked—it looked like the gulf with its water rising. Let the flood come. Let the flood come and we will swim.

Legs, legs, legs went the rise. Legs, legs, legs went the push. Legs, legs, legs went the pull. Arms, arms, arms went the wide, and arms, arms, arms went the divide.

There was trickling down our foreheads and there was trickling down the backs of our necks. The trickling went on and on and on, and we stood there like we were nothing, and the trickling was everything.

Far away, there was distance, and the distance kept coming, and we waited. And we ran. And we stopped. There was singing. There were lips.

We kissed there, and the metal thumped, and the clouds went away and came back. We found our way through each other. We dug our hands in pie and milk. We kept eating. We kept drinking. We never knew what this all meant and we never tried to know.

131

Wondering was what kept us going.

Dream, dream, dream went the eyes. Dream, dream, dream went the float. Up, up, up went the dream.

Our faces, red and wet and hot—we kept going until there was panting. Our naked bodies—we weren't free. We were just teasing ourselves until we stopped laughing. Or crying. Or hurting.

Out there, out in the sad field—it drooped and sagged—there was a chance for us to disappear. But we stayed. We were all stubborn.

BLUE AND GONE

Pepper was gone gone gone. We went looking for her—me and Ma and Barn. We went to town and we drove the country and we looked everywhere, but Pepper was gone gone gone.

Last time we had seen her was at night. We all stayed up late and talked in the living room eating midnight snacks. She ended up going to sleep in my bed, and Barn slept next to her.

In the morning, Barn was still there, but Pepper was gone gone gone. I looked for a note or a sign or anything but there wasn't anything. Barn was the note or the sign or anything. When Pierre had come over, and when Pepper said she felt bad about everything, I could tell she had Barn in mind. She didn't want anything to happen to Barn. She didn't want anything to happen to us, either, but Barn was the key. I didn't care if anything happened to me, but I would care if anything happened to Barn or Pepper or Ma, so I could see where she was coming from. I was sure Ma thought the same thing—she wouldn't care if anything happened to her, but Barn, me, and Pepper—she did.

We spent the day and the night looking for her. We went to the grocery store to see if The Dirty Man would pop up. Nothing. We went to the jazz club and the gardening center and the bowling alley. Nothing. We drove across all the fields near our house but she wasn't there. I gave Ma directions to Pepper's old house, not telling her that it was Pepper's old house, but she wasn't there. The red truck was nowhere to be seen.

Ma said, Maybe she left town.

Maybe the town left her, I said.

Ma nodded.

She wouldn't, I said.

Ma said, She's probably handling her business right now.

To keep us safe, I said.

Barn was tapping on the window, and Ma put it down so Barn could stick his hands out. Then he stuck his head out. I did the same. I thought about Pepper doing the same when I was driving her around town the other day. The air was making me close my eyes, and the hot air pounded against my skin. It made me feel hopeless.

Be good, I said. I said, Pepper.

Ma said, Be good.

When we got back to the house we searched everywhere there, too. Maybe she just went out for the day, but she wasn't there. She wasn't in the attic or the barn or in the garage or on the roof or anything.

Barn went to his room and sat on the floor with his back against the wall. He stretched out his legs and arms and then he looked under his bed. He pulled out a lunchbox full of his drawings and watercolors. There was one just of Pepper. She was naked and holding a flower. And there was a sun and a bird and everything else was blue.

I said, Blue and gone.

Barn flapped his arms like a bird.

WHEN BARN FLEW

I thought I heard someone coming inside the house so I got out of bed, hoping it was Pepper. The house was dark and quiet and empty. Barn wasn't in his room, and Ma was in her room, sleeping.

Outside, there were only bug sounds. With the glare of the street light, I could see Barn's leg dangling over the roof.

I said, Barn.

His head popped up. His hair was messy and his eyes were barely open.

I said, You could fall.

Barn waved.

I got onto the roof and pulled Barn away from the edge.

I said, Where are you going.

Barn flapped his arms.

I said, In the morning. I said, You can't fly on an empty stomach. I said, Wait for breakfast and then go.

Barn rubbed his stomach.

I said, Where's Pepper.

He looked away, out onto the field.

I said, Go find Pepper.

Barn stood up. I held his hand. He broke free and started to run.

I said, Fuck.

Barn kept running.

I said, Slow down Barn.

He was getting near the edge again.

I said, Wake up.

Barn left the roof. His legs weren't touching anything. He arms were up in the air. He head was looking up. He went forward and forward and forward and up and up and up. He was flying and gliding. For those few seconds, Barn was in the air and there was nothing around him. For those few seconds, nothing could touch him and he was flying. Barn was gone.

I looked over the roof. There was Barn on the ground—on his back, facing me with a smile.

I said, Barn. I said, You flew.

He waved.

I said, You're hurt.

Barn flapped his arms.

I said, You flew.

He took a few seconds to stand up. He limped a bit as he walked around the yard.

I said, How did it feel.

Barn stretched out his arms and moved around in the grass. He was smiling. He stopped and looked up at the moon. I didn't notice it until Barn looked at it. It was large and round. It looked pretty close to the earth.

I said, You were there.

He tried to grab the moon. I closed one eye and framed the moon between my fingertips.

I said, Cookie.

I stood up and stretched my legs.

I said, Should I try.

Barn zipped around and looked up at me. He put out his arms.

I said, You'll catch me.

I went back all the way to the other end, as much as possible. I was at the tip—a bit closer to the moon, a bit closer to nothing. I took one step, and then another, and then ran as fast as possible. I was in the air.

While I was in the air, I saw a trail of sparks screeching past me. There was a red truck. It was swerving and glowing. Barn pointed at it. I hit the ground.

Road, road, road went the spark. Truck, truck, truck went the red. Barn, Barn, Barn went the point. Tire, tire, tire went the screech. Ground, ground, ground, went the ankles. Umph, umph, umph went the body. Scream, scream, scream went the throat.

Everything was dizzy.

Roll, roll, roll went the world. World, world, world went the spin. Go, go, go went the engine.

Barn came up to me and helped me stand. The ankle was in pain. We were both limping. I looked down the road, and I could still see the truck screeching and sparking and swerving. It went onto the field, towards the barn. Another car sped by. Its engine was loud and honking. There was a smell of rubber. It kept going onto the field, following the red truck.

I said, barn. I said, Barn.

There went another car—it wasn't going as fast. It couldn't go as fast. It was an old car. There was smoke coming from the hood. It shrieked and dragged along slowly, but it also went onto

136

the field, following the other car and the truck, towards the barn.

I went inside to get Ma. She was in a good snore.

I said, Ma.

Ma snored. I shook her. She turned around and pushed me away. I shook her.

I said, Ma.

Ma woke up and sneezed.

Allergies, Ma said.

I said, Storm.

Ma got out of bed and fixed her muumuu.

I said, Barn.

Ma said, Barn.

I said, Front yard.

We started walking.

Ma said, You're limping.

I said, Barn flew.

Ma said, Let him go.

We got outside and Barn was gone. Me and Ma drove onto the field towards the barn. The front part was halfway down. There was a crash, and the red truck was jutting out of the barn, covered in smoke and wood and hay. The second car had ran into it, and the front part came crashing down. The smaller car was parked right near the entrance.

Ma ran in ahead of me. I was limping behind. We didn't have any defense with us, and I hoped that Pepper still had the gun. There were these loud noises and shouting and screaming and cursing. There were clanks and crashes and tings and tangs and there was hay flying around everywhere. There were bocks and meows and moos, and there were nays and baaas and bleats.

There was a bear. There were horses. There was Horse. There was swarming and buzzes, and there was smoke filling up the barn.

There was The Dirty Man. There was the mumbling man mumbling. There was Pepper. Pepper was in blood. Her head had gashes. There were birds in the air, and there was a fire.

Ma said, Why is there a bear.

Zoo, I said.

It must have escaped.

Ma said, Why is there a fire.

Pierre was there. They were bunched up in the corner, standing around Pepper.

Ma said, Damn it Pierre.

Pierre waved.

You got two chickens, I said.

Pierre waved.

Ma said, You ready.

I grabbed a shovel. Ma grabbed the wheelbarrow. We took off and ran into The Dirty Man, the mumbling man, and Pierre.

Everyone went to the ground. Pepper was already on the ground. Pepper was in blood. Pepper was in a daze.

I said, Pepper.

Pepper looked at me with no eyes. She had no mouth. Her face was red and her body was red and she wasn't there.

I said, Pepper.

Pepper tried to get up, but she stumbled and fell back down. Pepper was mumbling.

I said, What.

Pepper was mumbling.

I said, What.

The Dirty Man was in the wheelbarrow. Pierre was on his stomach. The mumbling man was on his side. Everything was dizzy and the sounds were all blurry.

The bear was on its fours looking at the chickens. The cows and the horses were shuffling around. The goats and sheep were loose and they ran away.

Ma grabbed a wooden board and raised it above her head, looking down on The Dirty Man in the wheelbarrow.

The Dirty Man still looked out of it. Ma swung the board down on The Dirty Man's chest and the wooden board splintered and The Dirty Man screamed. The mumbling man came about and tackled Ma.

I said, Ma.

I looked at Pepper. Her eyes were closed and her head was leaning against the wall. A chicken strolled past us. Pepper whimpered. I tackled the mumbling man. The Dirty Man shouted.

Mallow, The Dirty Man said.

The employee ran into the barn.

I said, Where'd you come from.

He ran to The Dirty Man and helped him out of the wheelbarrow. The mumbling man got a hold of my head.

Punch, punch, punch went the fist.

The Dirty Man got on top of me.

Punch, punch, punch went the fist. I was flailing my arms and then there was nothing.

Pierre, The Dirty Man, and the mumbling man were scuffling. The mumbling man went back to Ma. She was still on the ground.

There went a turtle.

I said, Turtle.

The mumbling man kicked Ma. Pepper whimpered. Her eyes were open. She moved her head from side to side. The Dirty Man went over to her and grabbed her by the hair. I felt a hand on my back and turned around and swung. It was Pierre.

I'm good, Pierre said.

I took another swing.

No, Pierre said.

He stepped back and put his hands up.

I'm good, Pierre said.

I said, Let's go.

We were all fighting. Pierre went over to the mumbling man. I went over to The Dirty Man and the employee, crashing both of them into the wall. The bear growled. There were bocks. We were all swinging. There were hits. I hit. I got hit. The Dirty Man slammed Pepper's head against the ground. Hay flew. My foot went between the employee's legs, and the employee cried and crouched and went to the ground. There was one more hit, and his eyes were closed.

Pierre and the mumbling man were wrestling. I took the shovel and swung at The Dirty Man. I missed. Pierre was on the ground. The Dirty Man kicked. I was on the ground. I was face to face with Pepper. Her eyes were closed again.

I said, I love you.

There were slashes. My skin tore. My arms and legs split open. There was leaking blood. There was a blade.

I said, I love you.

There was Ma on the ground. The mumbling man was pushing her face into the hay.

I said, I love you.

I tried to get back up but there was more force and I was ready to go. I saw all of these things. I saw a bear and some cows, and I saw chickens, and a turtle. I saw hay and baaaas and bleats. I saw red and I saw sparks and I saw heat. There were The Dirty Man's boots. I saw a torn muumuu and I saw words. I saw ants, and there was a bee. I saw fields over fields over fields, bronze and flowing, and I saw the wind and the sun, and everything was twinkling. There was a bird and it was in the air, looking at me with gentle eyes and a long smooth beak. It opened its beak and it said something I could hear. I saw mute. I saw fireflies and lightning bugs and I saw a red truck and a microphone. I saw Pepper's nipples and her thighs, and I saw her mouth around me, and I saw my eyes were closed. I saw the ceiling fan and the toaster, and I saw the goat. I saw Pepper's tongue swirling around in my mouth. I saw Ma smoking a cigarette and falling asleep. I saw the chimney. I saw Barn. Barn was in the air. I saw Barn, and he was in the air with the biggest smile. He was flying here and there, and his arms flapped and we were all on his wings.

There was Barn. He came through the window. He was in the air. He landed on The Dirty Man. Hay flew. The bear looked at us. The chickens were all quiet. Horse was still there, trying to soothe us with her soft moos.

What the fuck, The Dirty Man said.

Barn took the knife from The Dirty Man's hand.

What the fuck, The Dirty Man said.

I said, Stab him.

Barn stabbed The Dirty Man in the thigh.

I said, Stab him.

Barn took out the knife from The Dirty Man's thigh and stabbed him again in the thigh. The Dirty Man closed his eyes and looked up and screamed. The bear started to walk out of the barn.

I said, Bye bear.

The mumbling man was beating on Ma. The Dirty Man shouted his name.

Mallow, The Dirty Man said.

I said, Pepper.

Pepper was nowhere. Her head was gone.

I said, Wake up.

Barn was having fun with The Dirty Man.

I said, Stab him.

The Dirty Man swung his arm and knocked Barn over. He landed next to Pepper. He didn't cry or shout or anything. He ran his fingers through Pepper's hair and nudged her shoulders. I turned back around and Pierre was trying to get the mumbling man off Ma.

I said, Pepper. I said, It's your dad.

She moved her head around and opened her eyes. She patted Barn on the head. She started to sing. It was a farm song about pigs and cows and goats. Her voice was strong. The barn was full of voice.

Barn got back up and started running circles around The Dirty Man. The Dirty Man kicked Barn. I kicked The Dirty Man. Barn stabbed The Dirty Man in the thigh. The Dirty Man was on the ground. The employee tried to get back up and I knocked him back down. I wrapped his body in rope and tied it to a stall post. He was done for the night.

Barn was trying to help Pepper to get up. I ran over to Pierre and the mumbling man and Ma. Ma was still on the ground, face first. Her head was buried in hay. I pulled her out. The mumbling man was taking Pierre left and right. Pierre didn't have a chance, but was giving all of us a break by distracting the mumbling man. The Dirty Man was rolling around on the ground. Pepper was standing up and leaning against the wall. Horse was looking at us.

I said, Ma. I said, You look good.

My muumuu is all torn up, Ma said.

I said, We can get you another one.

You know you were born during a hurricane, Ma said.

I said, Let's get you out of here.

This all makes sense, Ma said.

I said, Did you see the bear.

You were made to have a life of storms, Ma said.

I said, It was growling.

I'm sorry, Ma said.

It must have been about seven feet big, I said.

That's a big bear, Ma said.

Pepper's song filled our ears.

141

She has a beautiful voice, Ma said.

I said, Pretty.

Barn ran up to us and started to pet Ma. Ma patted him on the back.

I said, Barn.

I patted him on the head.

I said, You did good.

Barn hopped.

I said, You flew.

Pierre was shouting. The mumbling man was on top of him, trying to strangle him. As I was trying to get to them, Pepper tackled the mumbling man and started throwing punches. One after another after another, Pepper was giving it all she had. I could barely recognize her face—the blood and the messy hair covered her skin. Pepper kept beating him up until the mumbling man was able to shove her away.

Pepper said, Leave.

Sweetie, the mumbling man said.

His voice was hoarse and scratchy.

This is just business, the mumbling man said.

I will kill you, Pepper said.

Your dad, the mumbling man said. Your father, the mumbling man said. What would your mother say, the mumbling man said.

I will kill you, Pepper said.

Be a good daughter, the mumbling man said. Be a good daughter, the mumbling man said. And listen to your father, the mumbling man said. The one man who took care of you and grew you up, the mumbling man said.

Pepper pulled out her gun. The mumbling man pulled out his gun. Pepper pointed her gun at the mumbling man. The mumbling man pointed his gun at Barn. I stood in front of Barn.

All the same, the mumbling man said.

Pepper said, Dad.

Sweetie, the mumbling man said.

Pepper said, I'll go with you. Pepper said, Let's just go. Pepper said, Let's just let them go.

You'll do good, the mumbling man said. But, the mumbling man said. They have to be gone, the mumbling man said.

He cocked the pistol. Pepper cocked the pistol. Pierre came in from behind and tackled the mumbling man. A gun went off.

I said, Who shot.

The Dirty Man was hobbling around now, cursing and groaning.

All this just for a little action, The Dirty Man said.

The mumbling man said, You shut it.

Pierre was on the ground. There was a hole in his stomach. There was leaking blood.

Ma said, Pierre.

Pierre said, Laurennette.

Your girl is a no good, The Dirty Man said.

The Dirty Man hobbled up to the mumbling man and Pepper. He slapped Pepper across the face.

Be a good girl, the mumbling man said.

The Dirty Man said, Listen to your Pops. The Dirty Man said, Be a good girl.

It's for the best, the mumbling man said.

I went over to Pierre. Ma was already there.

Pierre said, You're my sperm.

Ma put the back of her hand against Pierre's forehead.

Pierre said, But I'm glad I didn't raise you.

Ma put the back of her hand against Pierre's neck.

Pierre said, I would have messed you up.

Ma put her hand on top of the hole to keep the blood from coming out.

Pierre said, I was useless but I'm proud of you.

Pierre closed his eyes and his chest stopped moving. I looked at Ma and there were tears.

The mumbling man stood there with the gun and watched his daughter being slapped by The Dirty Man.

This is for the best, the mumbling man said.

The Dirty Man said, Your Pops wants to stay alive. The Dirty Man said, Your Pops wants to stay alive.

You must suffer, the mumbling man said.

The gun fell out of Pepper's hand. Barn picked it up. He had a knife in one hand and a gun in the other hand. Ma kissed Pierre's nose. She was sweating, and there was blood all around her.

Barn threw the knife at the mumbling man and it hit him in the arm. The mumbling man cursed.

Pepper said, Good shot.

Shoot him, I said.

Barn shot The Dirty Man.

The bullet hit him in the stomach.

143

Shoot him, I said.

Pepper said, Shoot him.

Be good, Ma said.

Barn ran over to Pepper and gave her the pistol. She cocked it and aimed it at The Dirty Man. The mumbling man, mumbling and cursing, aimed his gun at Pepper.

It's good money, the mumbling man said.

The Dirty Man said, If I'm gone, we're all gone.

Pepper looked at Barn. Pepper looked at Ma. Pepper looked at me. Pepper shot her dad. Pepper shot her dad twice. Pepper's dad fell to the ground and there was silence and smoke.

I tackled The Dirty Man. I picked up the blade. We are all together. Everyone was shot and stabbed and beaten and kicked and on the ground.

Woozy.

I knifed The Dirty Man.

Blade, blade, blade went the skin. Pierce, pierce, pierce went the bullet. Torn, torn, torn went the muumuu. Dead, dead, dead went the body. Dead, dead, dead went the body. Pierre, Pierre, Pierre went Mallow. Mallow, Mallow, Mallow went Pierre.

There were closed eyes and shuffling and moaning. The animals were quiet—we were an event.

Stab. Leak. Grunt. Twist.

The knife goes in easy with hatred. The Dirty Man didn't say a word. He breathed in hard and he let go of his breath.

Pepper stood there looking at all of us like the animals. Mallow. The mumbling man. Pepper's dad had hay in his hands. His arms across his body—Barn nudged the mumbling man for signs of life.

The Dirty Man was there on the ground looking up. His lips were red and his shirt was red. His boots were caked in dirt and manure.

Fuck, The Dirty Man said.

There was a moo. Good Horse and her moo. Ma brushed off her muumuu and walked away from Pierre, towards The Dirty Man. She stood over him and stared into his eyes. The Dirty Man stared back. The Dirty Man closed his eyes. The Dirty Man gave in.

Barn held Pepper's hand and guided her towards Mallow. Pepper knelt down and patted his chest. Pepper knelt down and touched his skin. There were tears and there was tearing. Pepper wanted to see the holes. They were through the chest. She covered him in hay and Barn helped her.

The fires had calmed. The smoke was thin. We all looked at the barn opening—half crashed in and full of dented cars and flat tires. I looked at the bear prints that led out of the barn.

Some storm, Ma said.

We all sat down, leaning against the wall, in a row—in a line—and tilted our heads back. There was nothing said. I closed my eyes. I opened my eyes. I closed my eyes. I opened my eyes and Barn was gone. He flew back to where he came from. Barn, the flying being, who came and went, taking care of us all. The silent guardian with his invisible cape had gone to save another earth.

Ma stood up and started cleaning. She brushed the hay back into the corner. She fixed the doors of the stalls and petted the animals. None of them were shot or stabbed—they were all good.

That was some bear, I said.

Ma said, It must have gotten out from the zoo.

It'll find a place, I said.

I put the gates back on their hinges. I pushed the cars out of the way. We hosed down the remnants of the fire and we hosed down ourselves. There was pain. There was stinging. We had wounds and aches.

Ma said, We're going to need a lot of rubbing alcohol.

And alcohol, I said.

Pepper was still gone. She hadn't said a word as she remained sitting and looking at the barn before her. Her eyes were watery and red. Her skin was watery and red. There was sweat and there were scrapes.

You'll be good, I said.

Pepper looked at me. She rubbed her arms. She rolled her head around and stretched her neck. I helped her up and she helped us clean. Every now and then, she would stop and look at the mumbling man, Mean Mallow Marsh, her dad. Every now and then, she was gone and away, looking out of the barn. I looked out with her, past the brightness and into the darkness.

What are you thinking, I said.

I couldn't see her thoughts, but I imagined she was in the back. She was in the past, when she was just a little girl, holding her parents' hands as they walked through a field full of green and yellow.

You can sing, I said.

I thought about Pierre. I thought about Pierre and Ma, and I looked at Ma who stood there looking at Pierre. I imagined she was in the back. She was in the past, picturing her, and Pierre, and me by the river with our fishing poles and tackle boxes. There was a time when he was there, and we were all together, and there were bits of memories.

There was a nice time, I said.

Ma nodded her head. She took the can of dip out of Pierre's pocket and kept it with her.

Ma said, When everything was good.

A DRINK

There were twirling lights and blues and reds. There were sirens and uniforms and questions. It took them a long time to find the place. We stayed in the barn until they got there. Pepper fell asleep on a stack of hay. Ma kept looking at Pierre. I kept thinking about the bear.

There were more questions, and they said that there will be more questions. Both The Dirty Man and Mean Mallow Marsh had a lot of warrants and records. They seemed relieved that they were all dead, and that we were all alive. There was still the employee. The last we saw of him was when the officer pushed his head down as he got into the backseat of the police car.

Self-defense, I said.

Ma said, The barn is our home.

Before they got there, I took off all of the fingerprints—the blade and the gun, making sure that none of it could be traced back to Barn. He would have been okay, but it would have been too much of a hassle with the police trying to question him because Barn didn't talk. He just flew.

When it was all done, the morning had come, and there was the sun, and there was the rooster's crow, and there was the newspaper. The front page had an article about an escaped bear. The tigers could have escaped, too, said the article, but they remained at their stations. I had carried Pepper back from the car to the living room. Her head sagged and her arms were limp. I put my ear to her chest and listened to her breathe.

Sing, I said.

The ambulance at the barn had fixed us up with gauze pads and bandages and rubbing alcohol. Ma got out the other kind of alcohol and we sat out on the porch and looked at the dew.

How do we go to sleep, Ma said.

I said, There's a lot of ringing.

It'll mute, Ma said

There was a leg dangling over the roof.

Ma said, Look.

Barn, I said.

The legs left. The head appeared.

Sleep, I said.

The head disappeared. He came out from the back and gave

147

Ma a hug. He gave me a hug. I kissed him on the forehead.

Sleep, I said.

He went inside.

Ma said, That's a good kid.

She was in the rocking chair—it squeaked in rhythm.

Ma said, Pepper is a good girl.

She's a good girl, I said.

Ma said, We're all together.

Strange, I said.

We sat there on the porch and looked onto the road. The mailbox was broken. There were screech marks on the road. My ankle hurt. I had forgotten that I tried to fly like Barn. The sky was there and it was pink and edible. The sun was gorgeous. It was warming and caring.

I looked at Ma, and she had fallen asleep on the rocking chair. I went inside and got a blanket and covered her, and I sat there on the bench next to her looking at the front yard. There was this grasshopper jumping around. And there was this ladybug on my thumb. And in the air, there was this gliding bird—it's wings weren't moving, but it kept going until the sun blinded it.

The lady in the jean shorts wore a long black dress. It was slim, and her body was there. There were just a few of us. The lady in the jean shorts put flowers on the coffin. Ma didn't cry. Barn didn't cry. Pepper was there and she didn't cry. It was a good morning.

Ma rubbed the coffin and whispered something and walked away. I went up to Pierre and tapped the wood. Barn held Pepper's hand and they walked up and they touched the wood. Ma went up to the lady in the jean shorts.

Ma said, You're a good girl.

You know, the lady in the jean shorts said. He talked about you a lot, the lady in the jean shorts said. You all, the lady in the jean shorts said.

She turned towards me and put her hand on my shoulder.

He regretted, the lady in the jean shorts said. But he knew it was for the best, the lady in the jean shorts said.

Ma said, He had that look in his eyes. Ma said, A look I hadn't seen in years. Ma said, There was something there.

We all went back to the house and ate fried chicken. Ma showed the lady in the jean shorts how to boil crawfish, too. We stayed home all day until the sun went down, drinking beer and laughing. It was nice to see Pepper laughing. It was a free laugh. It was a loud laugh, too, and sometimes she laughed so loud, there were tears coming down her cheeks. Barn would wipe them away.

It's okay, Pepper said. They're good, Pepper said.

Ma went on and on telling stories about Pierre. The lady in the jean shorts would nod her head. She knew exactly what Ma was talking about. It was something that both of them could relate to. It was first time I really learned about the dad I never had. He had his bad ways, but the good ways also stuck out. And I was glad he wasn't there for me. And I was glad that we were able to say bye to each other.

Me and Pepper went off into the night, to the field. She held my hand and we hunched against the tractor listening to the bugs again and looking at the stars.

I said, Let's go riding around.

We got into the tractor and bumped along the field. The quietness of the place was broken with the rattling of the engine and the sound of diesel. We breathed in hard.

Pepper said, Let's get out.

I turned off the engine.

Pepper said, Leave the headlights on.

I switched them on.

Pepper said, I want to be able to see you.

She took her dress off and put it on the hood of the tractor. In the headlights, she was surrounded by mosquitoes but they looked like fireflies, and Pepper looked like she was glowing. Her body curved in the dark and in the light. She took off her bra and put it on the hood of the tractor. Her nipples poked out into the light. Her breasts were up and they looked gentle. She took off her underwear and folded it and put it on the hood of the tractor, and Pepper was naked in the dark and in the light, and her skin blended with the air, and I could see her with my eyes closed.

She came up to me and took off my shirt. She unbuckled my belt and unzipped my jeans. I lifted one leg and then the other. She pulled down my underwear and I stepped over it. She took my clothes and put them on the hood of the tractor.

Pepper said, I want to be able to see you.

There was a rabbit.

We licked each other's scabs and felt each other's bruises and pushed on these points to make us hold our breaths. Pepper's hands were searching my skin, and my tongue looked for teeth.

Pepper held me and moved me up and down. With my eyes closed, I could see her. There was a soft moan from Pepper. She put my hands on her chest and told me to pet her heart.

Our ribs pressed in and out—they wore so sore and in need of pillows, and we lay in the grass and rubbed ourselves in the blades. The headlights shined on as we rolled around trying to get hold of each other. Pepper's nose. Pepper's thighs. Pepper's fingers and toes. They were all in my mouth. We scratched the back of each other's necks and arms, and Pepper was quiet.

I couldn't see her eyes but I knew they were there. Pepper was there, and there were glimpses of the rabbit. It sat there, and it was just us.

There was a slit. It was open and wet and I went in. It was familiar and strange—a feeling of being home after being away for so long. When she was on top of me, I put my hands on her hips and pinched her skin. Her hands ran through her own hair, and there was a shadow of two being one.

When I was on top of her, I was close to her breath and licked her chin, and she stayed still and kept her legs wide, and her hands were around me, digging deep into my spine.

Sometimes I was behind her, and she looked back at me, and I looked at her, and our eyes were closed. And when we were done, she ran her hands across my chest, and I held her close so I could smell her mud and soil and grass. And she looked at me.

Who are you, Pepper said.

I said, Pepper.

I am Mutty, Pepper said.

I said, We know each other.

Don't leave, Pepper said.

I said, We are Pepper and Mutty.

And the rabbit left.

We were at the correctional center. Ma was dressed up, too. She wore a dress and Pepper helped her with her makeup. Her lips were really red and her cheeks were full of blush and her eyelashes were long and curly.

It'll be nice, Pepper said.

Ma said, We should look good for him.

Presentable, I said.

Pepper looked pretty—she was wearing nice gray pants and a dark blue button-up shirt. Ma helped me tie a tie and I tucked in my shirt. Barn didn't have a tie, but he wore a shirt with a collar. We all looked good, and I looked at Pepper.

I said, You look pretty.

You look nice, Pepper said.

We sat on one side of the glass window. Uncle Gerald showed up. He was wearing all orange. His hair was growing back, and his eyes weren't red and his eyebrows were thin. He smiled as he sat down and he didn't look so mean as he did when he was in the newspaper.

Barn jumped and skipped, and Ma had to put him in her lap to keep control of him

They might put you in jail for disturbing the peace, Ma said.

Barn started tapping on the window, and Uncle Gerald tapped back. Ma picked up the phone.

Brother, Ma said.

I looked at Uncle Gerald and read his lips, and it looked like he said sister. Ma told Uncle Gerald about everything that had happened, and Uncle Gerald looked through the window at us with huge eyes. Sometimes, his eyes were narrow, too.

But it's all okay, Ma said.

I got on the phone.

Uncle Gerald said, You did good.

I said, Barn did good, too.

Uncle Gerald said, Take care of him,

I said, He's taking care of us.

Uncle Gerald said, Come visit more.

I said, It'll be good.

I gave the phone to Barn. He held the phone upside down. Pepper flipped it around for him. He put a finger in his other ear so he could hear. He didn't look at Uncle Gerald at first—he just looked down. Every now and then he smiled, and Uncle Gerald was laughing. Sometimes Barn would move the phone away from his ear and look at it like he was trying to figure out how his dad's voice was coming out from it. We couldn't tell what he was saying to Barn but it looked fun as they both looked cheerful. Our time was up, and we had to go. Uncle Gerald's eyes were watery. Ma's eyes were watery. Barn looked curious, and his eyes were wide and open.

Bye Daddy, Barn said.

We all looked at Barn, and he was flying in the air.

Thank You: Many thanks to all of the editors and literary journals who have taken on excerpts from this novel in one form or another. Thank you, Joe Taylor and the Livingston Press staff for giving this novel a home. Thanks to all of my friends for always encouraging and supporting me to continue to write. Thank you, Louisiana, especially the city of Lafayette and the surrounding areas. And thanks to my parents, Sarmistha and Subrata Dasgupta, my brother, Deep, and Heidi for always being there.

Shome Dasgupta is the author of *i am here And You Are Gone* (Winner Of The 2010 OW Press Fiction Chapbook Contest), *The Seagull And The Urn* (HarperCollins India, 2013) which has been republished in the UK by Accent Press as *The Sea Singer* (2016), *Anklet And Other Stories* (Golden Antelope Press, 2017), and *Pretend I Am Someone You Like* (University of West Alabama's Livingston Press , 2018). His second collection of stories, *Mute*, is forthcoming from Tolsun Books. His stories and poems have appeared in *Puerto Del Sol, New Orleans Review, NANO Fiction, New Delta Review,Necessary Fiction, Magma Poetry*, and elsewhere. His fiction and poetry have been anthologized in *The &Now Awards 2: The Best Innovative Writing* (&Now Books, 2013) and *Poetic Voices Without Borders 2* (Gival Press, 2009). His work has been featured as a storySouth Million Writers Award Notable Story, nominated for The Best Of The Net, and longlisted for the Wigleaf Top 50. He lives in Lafayette, LA, and his website can be found at www.shomedome.com.